Oops. This one was a just little more than I could handle...

I wasn't alone. Vampire. Raw. Maybe a wild one. I looked up, nerves tingling because of the quick change to Kristen and back again. Saw him standing at one end of the alley, head turned to the side. Shakespeare's profile, with the firm brow and the long straight nose. Streetlights glistened on his curls. Very close, but not Shakespeare.

"I could tear your head off and let your blood mix with the bile and garbage and mud." His voice was Shakespeare's, too, but not quite. He moved enough to show the silhouette of the sword he was carrying.

I stood straighter, opened my arms a little. "Bring it."

"Bitch." He came at me too fast to see and smacked me across the face. My head hit the dumpster with a ringing crash. I landed on one knee, grateful I was in boots. Upright, Mr. Sticky and I had a chance. If he got me on the ground, I was done.

His shadow towered over me. "The moon's light begs mercy. She tells me to save you now that we might savor you together."

"So much like him, but not Shakespeare."

"Not Chaucer or Oscar Wilde, either, though they were both good men. I am Sir Hugh Robartes. You are nothing. You are dirt. You are dead."

"You're John's brother."

"Don't say that name."

His fist found my face again, knocking me back into the brick. I felt Mr. Sticky fly off into the shadows—then I was out.

She's a quiet, unassuming bookstore owner by day, but by night...

Kristen has a deadly secret—when she smells a vampire, she turns into Jai, a beauti-licious babe who makes vamps *permanently* dead. To a vamp, Jai is like ambrosia. They can't resist her. She uses this attraction, plus her super strength and her trusty blade, Mr. Sticky, to end their undead lives. The thrill of wearing miniskirts without worrying about cellulite stifles any qualms Kristen might have about killing the undead. Being Jai is the most fun she has ever had—until they come up against the *one* vampire Jai can't kill. If he and Jai have a history, as he claims, Jai can't remember it...or him.

But when her work catches the attention of some old enemies—who won't hesitate to destroy Kristen if it also means the end of Jai—this vampire may be their only hope. Can Kristen and Jai learn to tell the difference between good and evil in time to defeat Jai's ancient nemesis? Or will being Jai's hostess cost Kristen more than just her beauty sleep?

KUDOS FOR A VAMPIRE'S DEADLY DELIGHT

A Vampire's Deadly Delight is cute, funny, exciting, and sexy. It's short, which is good because once I started it, I couldn't put it down. And wouldn't you know, I started it on a night when I had to work the next day so I couldn't just relax and enjoy it. Bummer. But as it was short, it only kept me up for half the night, not all of it. Still, it was worth it...The plot was interesting and different, with enough twists and turns to keep me hooked, as the bags under my eyes attest. Plus there were some pretty hot sex scenes—well, almost sex scenes, I guess, since they didn't actually get to finish, but what was done was still pretty hot and steamy. All in all, A Vampire's Deadly Delight is a really fun read. — *Taylor, Reviewer*

A Vampire's Deadly Delight is a delightful paranormal romance/chick lit novella. Chick Lit isn't really my genre, but nevertheless, I found the book thoroughly enjoyable. It's cute, funny, intriguing, and the plot line is very different for a paranormal romance. The book has one heroine with two identities. Or should I say it has two heroines sharing the same body? Either way, the storyline is fresh and intriguing... The book is written in both third and first person, which although it's tricky to do, it is very well done. Our two heroines, Kristen and Jai, share Kristen's body as she is Jai's hostess—kind of a Clark Kent/Superman situation—and both of their POVs are in first person. But all the other POVs are in third person. I was impressed that while the publisher put Jai's and Kristen's POVs in different fonts to help the reader tell who was who, I could tell who was speaking from the voice of the character. It takes a good author to do that, and Rancourt appears to be a very good one. — *Regan, Reviewer*

A
VAMPIRE'S
DEADLY
DELIGHT

LIV RANCOURT

A BLACK OPAL BOOKS PUBLICATION

GENRE: Paranormal Romance/Chick-Lit

This is a work of fiction. Names, places, characters and incidents are either the product of the author's imagination or are used fictitiously, and any resemblance to any actual persons, living or dead, businesses, organizations, events or locales is entirely coincidental. All trademarks, service marks, registered trademarks, and registered service marks are the property of their respective owners and are used herein for identification purposes only. The publisher does not have any control over or assume any responsibility for author or third-party websites or their contents.

A VAMPIRE'S DEADLY DELIGHT
Copyright © 2011 by Liv Rancourt – All Rights Reserved
Cover Design by Liza Rancourt-Fennimore
Copyright © 2011 – All rights Reserved

Print ISBN: 978-1-937329-28-0

First publication: January 2012

Published by Black Opal Books **http://www.blackopalbooks.com**

ACKNOWLEDGMENTS

I would like to thank the editors and staff at Black Opal Books for taking a chance on a new author and for their exquisite patience with all my perambulations as I worked through this process.

I would also like to thank <u>all</u> of my sisters for their support and Snake for putting up with me.

CHAPTER 1

So when I came to, I was handcuffed to a bed. Someone had used old-fashioned metal cuffs—one on each limb—pinning me spread-eagle. All I could hear was the sound of my own heart pounding. The only illumination came from a single small candle. I rocked my head back to see what was behind me. The sickly light reflected off the twists and curves of an old brass headboard. Underneath me was what felt like a down comforter with a silky cover, and I was glad I'd worn a long dress to work, because even though the orange cotton made my round body look a bit like a pumpkin, I couldn't feel any inappropriately naked flesh. My feet were bare and I felt pretty green, but I had underpants on and whoever tied me up had left my bifocals, um, I mean, my progressive lenses in place. At least I'd be able to see whatever was coming to get me.

It occurred to me that it would be hours before anyone missed me. Robbie was right, there were situations when it would be handy to have a man at home. Too bad I was so stubbornly single. I tried to blink back my tears because it really didn't seem like crying would help. I was nearly at the silent sobbing stage when I was distracted by the sound of a door opening. There was a puff of rose perfume, then a figure walked in carrying a candle. I recognized Vivienne, a frequent flyer at my bookstore who I'd more-or-less made friends with. I didn't know much more about her than that she had a preference for historical romances, which she found unaccountably funny, but seeing someone I recognized made me feel a little better. Only a little better.

Vivienne had always been kind of odd, a pale and insubstantial figure draped in flowing gowns, her auburn hair worn long and loose so that it fell in graceful tendrils around her face. When my hair was long and loose, it frizzed out so I looked like a milkweed pod. From the little I knew about Vivienne, I'd always figured that she'd played one too many games of Dungeons and Dragons. This must be one of those games.

"I'm so sorry, Kristen. I had to bring the Master a gift. He's refusing me."

"Right now I'd refuse you too." If I pressed my eyes shut I could remember her coming into the store right as I was closing up for the night.

"The Master needs to feed." She sounded like she might cry.

I had no idea what she was talking about. "I hope you at least locked up when we left."

"Of course," she said.

I guess I should be thankful for small favors. Finding an empty cash register in the morning would make it all that much worse. That's assuming I ever made it back to work.

"He comes," she whispered, holding the candle higher so that its light spilled over me.

"Vivienne, what is this?" The voice was deep, resonant, a perfect match for the man who came through the door. He was a modern update of a classic Greek hero, square jaw, strong nose, close-cropped golden curls and all. But—and this is significant—he smelled. Vampire. Dried meat left too long in the back cupboard mixed with old dirt and a hint of manure. Vampire.

This I could deal with.

I felt the change begin as soon as my mind registered his scent. My body got soft, like it was melting, and my legs stretched, shoulders broadened, and pudgy curves shifted into more strategic locations. My frizzy hair even calmed down, falling into loose waves that framed my temporary cheekbones. I wasn't Kristen anymore. I was Jai, a vampire's most deadly delight.

"You have loosed an asp in our bower," the vampire said softly.

Vivienne gasped. The chains snapped easily when I tugged at them. I was much stronger than Kristen.

"Your associates need to do better research, Shakespeare," I said, as I pried the cuffs from my wrists. They clanked onto the stone floor. I swung my legs around so I was sitting on the edge of the bed. I didn't need Kristen's bifocals, so the glasses were gone. I stood up in knee-high boots with what felt like 4-inch stilettos. I've always loved high heels. I think. My memory's not so great.

Kristen's pumpkin dress had morphed into a little peach-colored cotton top and pair of denim Daisy Dukes that put my flat tummy on proud display.

Nobody moved for a second while I worked off the ankle cuffs and adjusted my top. It would never do to flash The Girls at a dead guy before it was time.

"Dude, what's up?" I stalked towards him in a barely controlled surge of energy, letting those four inch heels put a sinuous swing into my step.

Vivienne held the candle, frozen in place. "I swear I did not know, Master."

The vampire was trying to poke holes in me with his eyes. I walked right up to him, pressing The Girls lightly into his chest. In my heels, I had maybe an inch on him, so I angled my gaze down until I met his amber eyes.

He didn't move, which was a little strange. Most vampires couldn't keep their hands off me, pawing at me like drunken high-school boys as soon as they got close enough.

"Don't you like me, Shakespeare?" I purred, my lips nearly touching his cheekbone.

"I will ask you but once, Jai. Please take a step back."

"Whoa, Shakespeare, no fair. You know my name, now you have to tell me yours."

He knew my name. How? I'd never met a vamp I didn't kill, so it's not like they introduced me to their friends. Only two people knew Jai and one of those was technically not a person. He was a large spider, and he was, well, my keeper. Or something. The other had been cuffed to the bed. I took a step back, which surprised me even more.

"Better."

In that one word I heard his tension, saw the wooden rigidity of his arms. Yeah, he wanted me. He wanted me bad. This one was strong. And old. As we stood, taking each other's measure, I could sense the power of his years on Earth. Woo baby, I'd never done one this old. Wasn't going to stop me, though. I reached for the short sword I kept in a sheath that was strapped to my thigh.

"Sorry we don't have time to catch up, Shakespeare baby," I said as I raised the blade I called Mr. Sticky. I imagined pressing it to his chest, making a quick slice up his sternum, right turn across his ribs, then back to make sure I got through his great vessels, the aorta and the vena cava. His heart would be mine. Too easy.

"Jai," he breathed.

I stood frozen in place, my normal protection against a vampire's vibe completely gone. They usually don't scare me. He did. He was so old, so powerful.

Pausing is always a mistake. It gave me time to really look at him. There was something warm, something good, worked into him, one golden thread in the blackened weave of his being. All I usually saw in a vampire was dead—bone and muscle, sinew and dust. This one was different. I didn't put Mr. Sticky away. I didn't go for his heart, either.

It was Vivienne who blinked first. She threw the candle at the bed then dove between me and the vampire. He grabbed at her hair. I heard a snap and saw her crumple to the floor, her neck making an awkward L-shaped curve, her head at an impossible angle to her shoulder. The candle went out and before I could respond I felt the vampire leave. Jai faded and Kristen came back.

I found myself standing barefoot in the dark with a dead woman, with no idea where Vivienne had hidden my Birkenstocks or how I'd get home. I shrugged and started forward slowly, feeling my way to the door. This was so not how I thought this day would end.

Sunrise didn't register in the subterranean room. Nevertheless, it triggered something in Vivienne, bringing her to consciousness as the morning light outside turned the clouds a soft mother-of-pearl. She still lay sprawled on the floor where she'd fallen, her head cocked at an unnatural angle. Slowly she blinked her eyes to clear them, then struggled to raise herself. Her mouth tasted like dust.

She made it up to her elbows, her head lolling loosely down her chest. When she was more or less upright, she put a hand over each ear and lifted. There was a sharp click as her head dropped into its normal place on her shoulders. She shook herself, flexing her neck and rolling her head from side to side, then untwisted the long chiffon skirt from around her legs. Satisfied, she stood and drifted towards the bed, feeling the cool and delicate silk against her legs as she moved.

Amber light pooled around the old gilded sconces that were evenly spaced along the bedroom wall. The spacious room was one of several constructed below a mid-century rambler in one of the older subdivisions northeast of Seattle.

She hated the house because Sir John had moved them there after hearing a rumor that someone was killing vampires. He had hoped that someone would be Jai. He'd guessed right.

From the street the house showed its age, though the basement rooms Sir John had renovated were luxurious. The stone floors were heated from below with a piped water system and the walls were heavy concrete that had been covered with tinted plaster, mahogany wainscoting, and stretches of heavy brocade fabric. There were no windows, and the door to the house above was kept locked.

Sir John, the vampire, was lying dead on the bed, his golden curls kissed gently by the light from the sconces and one hand clutching a chemise, its creamy silk turned a bitter tan by time.

Glaring at him, Vivienne tugged the chemise out of his hand. It had belonged to Jai in one of her past incarnations, though Vivienne doubted it would fit this new and buxom version. Sir John was Vivienne's, and she wouldn't share him again. It was too much for him to ask it of her. She was his Food, the one human he fed from and who he sustained indefinitely. Her hands pulled at the fragile silk, as if she would tear the old slip into pieces. She knew she would have to play along. She always did. She loved him. She'd just wait for her opportunity to chase Jai away. Again.

"You're here." Herbert scuttled out from behind the register as soon as I unlocked the door, his eight legs clicking on the glass countertop.

"No thanks to you." I crossed to the back of the store and hit the light switch. Pads of fluorescent tubes sprang into action above my head.

"That woman did something to you last night."

"And you did nothing to help." I was a little bitter.

"You look ok now." he said.

I glared at him. He was the size of a tea-cup poodle, which admittedly was big for a spider, but I could still step on him if he made me mad enough. He scooted back out of my way.

"Got lucky," I snapped. "She drugged me or spelled me or something so she could make a gift of me to her boyfriend."

"I always said you were a prize."

"Whatever. I hope you get spider mites."

Herbert climbed up onto the counter. "Tell me what happened."

"No."

"Please."

I shrugged. "It turned out the boyfriend was a vampire."

"Jai time," Herbert said.

"Right."

I opened the register. Yesterday's money was still in the till—which was a good thing—and I had time to drop yesterday's deposit at the bank before I opened for the day.

"Another heart for the collection."

"Or the trashcan." I was nervous about this next part so I gave myself a stern shake. "No, in fact, he got away." None of them had ever gotten away before.

"You let him get away?" Herbert was really being a pain.

"I didn't let him do anything."

"So the girlfriend helped."

"Not even. She ended up with her neck snapped. He was just real old and real strong. He kept himself from touching me. He knew my name."

I busied myself turning all the five-dollar bills so that Abraham Lincoln was facing the same direction. Remembering the vampire's response made me feel squidgy.

"No shit," Herbert said.

"Don't swear." It was automatic. I scolded him every time he swore. My parents raised me to believe that there were enough words in the English language that a person didn't need to use the dirty ones. "Even spiders don't need to use profanity."

"Well excuse me." Spiders didn't need to be sarcastic either, but that didn't stop Herbert. "So the big bad vamp didn't fall for your...assets?"

"The big bad vampire knew my name." I finished counting the bank into the register and slammed the door shut. "Kristen got chained to a bed by a vampire minion, Jai didn't get the tag, and poor Vivienne ended up with her neck broken. It was not a good night."

I headed into the back room faster than Herbert could crawl. Didn't want him to see me cry.

"Hey, come on. This guy must have a story. Let me check my sources."

"Sure, go consult your magic web."

I didn't look at him, just stared at the computer and kept plugging figures into the balance sheet. The bookkeeping was pretty easy. Once I entered all the cash and checks it would automatically add in all the debits and charges and compare it with the register tape. I could have worked faster except that I had to keep brushing away tears.

When I was done, I had time to run to the bank to deposit the cash and stop for some coffee before opening the store. I opened the office door and found that Herbert was planted in the middle of the aisle. He wasn't truly blocking me because I could easily have stepped over him. I stopped anyway, to be polite.

"Shoo. I need to work."

"This could be trouble," he said, his multifaceted eyes shining up at me.

He was so black that it was hard to see much of his face except for the glittering eyes and beak-like mouth. As it was, he looked like an oversized black widow with buckteeth and a thyroid condition. I stepped around him then walked through the long shelves of books, heading for the front door. I could hear him clicking along behind me.

"Only two vamps have shown any immunity to Jai," he said. "One keeps trying to kill her."

"That must be the reason you have to keep finding new recruits." Fine, I was willing to air all the dirty laundry today if he was. "Besides, I'm still alive, so maybe this is the other one."

"Jai is not a death sentence," he said.

I stared hard at him, trying to see if he had his fingers, or rather, his legs crossed. "Sure," I agreed and let myself out the front door.

CHAPTER 2

If Jai wasn't a death sentence, what was she? Only the most excitement I'd ever had. Before Jai, I'd never known what it felt like to have guys stare at me. I was just over thirty years old and never had much to do with men. Except for a couple of near misses, I'd been single my whole life. My best friend Robbie and I had been roommates until she got married. In the months leading up to her wedding I got tired of her frequent attempts to fix me up with Doug's friends. We had weekly, sometimes daily, conversations that went something like this.

Robbie: "He's cute."

Me: "I'm not interested."

Robbie: "You can't be single forever."

Me: "Or maybe I can."

Robbie: "This is because of your father, isn't it?"

Me: "No."

Robbie: "Just because he drank too much and fooled around on your mother…"

Me: "And ran off when I was thirteen."

Robbie: "And ran off when you were thirteen, and then in high school Rich Morgan didn't ask you out."

Me: "In high school Rich Morgan flirted with me for four months then asked Susie Upchuck, my formerly best friend, to Prom."

Robbie: "Susie Upchurch is a nice girl."

Me: "Remind me why you and I are friends."

Robbie: "You had your last date in college."

Me: "Yep."

Robbie: "And he turned out to be a scoundrel. So what? We all get involved with someone like that when we're in college. It's in the requirements next to English 100 and French 201."

Me: "I never took French."

Robbie: "Maybe you should have. Then you wouldn't be hanging around waiting for Mr. Darby or Heathcliff or whoever it is you're obsessing over this week."

That's usually when I walked out of the room. In my mind, I suffered from a clear case of "three strikes and you're out." When Robbie got married I missed her, though I didn't miss the constant pressure to get out there and meet someone.

The first night I sat down to dinner by myself, I raised a glass and promised I'd stay single. I liked me life and didn't feel compelled to share it with anyone. My grandfather left me some money when he died, and I used it to buy the bookstore where I'd worked in college. It wasn't in a great location, so when I saw the new mall opening, I moved the store. For the first couple of years I worked there by myself, only closing on Mondays and holidays. It wasn't a lifestyle that lent itself to dating. When it got busy enough, I hired

Robbie to come work with me in the store. Despite her frequent pep-talks, I still didn't look for a real man.

Real men always suffered when I compared them with whichever fictional character I was infatuated with. It started with Frank Hardy. He was darkly handsome and more thoughtful than his brother Joe. I was ten when I decided to marry him. It didn't last. A brief flirtation with Almanzo Wilder ended when I met Mr. Rochester. For about five months I looked everywhere for a bitter, brooding, older man that I could save with my youthful purity. In hindsight it was probably fortunate that I was unsuccessful. After Mr. Rochester was Aragorn, though I admit that my original vision of that character has been completely obliterated by Viggo Mortensen, who was fairly perfect in the movie version.

In high school I spent a few weeks riding through the French countryside with Athos and D'Artagnon and spent a hauntingly lovely weekend with Max de Winter. I would spend hours staring deeply into my own navel with Homer Wells. I rode dragons on Pern and found that bonding with a dragon was just as orgasmic as it was supposed to be. The summer after high school, I started to work in the bookstore, where I was always able to find someone new.

Along the way I met a few vampires. Don Ysidro was my first. His reserved sensuality intrigued me. Then I met Lestat, who truly captured my heart. I count the Vampire Lestat as one of my great loves. His energy, honesty, and radiant flair blazed through me. I was thrilled with his passion and the incredible depth of his feelings. While I knew in my heart that Lestat would never really care for a bookish woman with a caustic tongue, in my dreams I was slender and amusing. And beautiful. Unlike with Aragorn, I never confused the literary Lestat with the Tom Cruise version. Sorry, Tom. More recently I met Eric Northman, a sunnier, straighter cousin of Lestat who would probably laugh at my jokes. He's my current main vampire squeeze.

Or, more accurately, Eric was my current main literary vampire. In real life, I squeezed whichever vampire brought Jai out of me. I squeezed them and often kissed them and once or twice rode bareback on them. And I stabbed them, or rather Jai did. When I thought about it too long, it took my breath away. It was all so much fun. Yeah, unless Herbert was totally lying to me, it would be a while before I was tired of playing hostess for Jai.

After I dropped the bank deposit, I stopped at one of the mall's two Starbuck's locations to get some coffee. I really hoped that I'd reached my drama quotient for the day. I had plenty of customers and UPS brought a large-ish delivery I had to unpack. Herbert stayed hidden in his secret spider hidey-hole, so I didn't have him to impede me from getting things done. I was feeling pretty mellow—until I had to take out two vamps on my way home.

I was headed for the bus when I smelled the first one. He was strolling along pretending to shop while he looked for a meal. Could be he really was looking at the selection in the windows of Wilson's Leather? Not. I ducked behind a big sign that showed a map of the mall. Jai came out dressed in a black cat suit with glossy CFM pumps.

☠

I loved the outfit. It was always a thrill to move around in the stretchy black fabric and feel my bum up high and my thighs in tight. Oh yeah.

I coughed. Nothing. Glanced in the vampire's direction. He saw me looking. I started walking slowly towards a dark corner. He was closing in. When he was nearly on me I turned to face him.

"Hey Junior, you're crowding me," I said, pulling my shoulders back. Yeah, he was checking out the merchandise. He closed the gap between us quicker than I could see.

"So pretty," he said as he pulled me close.

His hands covered my breasts, finding nipple through the thin spandex. I always gave them a minute to play before Mr. Sticky, well, stuck. Guess I'm not above a cheap thrill. This one had long wavy black hair and the cutest little soul patch under his lip. He'd been young when he got turned, and he hadn't been a vampire long. I leaned into him, gently biting his lower lip right above the little tuft of surprisingly soft hair.

It was sad, really.

He came in closer, aiming for my neck. Before he could sink his teeth in, I had the blade in my hand. Up, right, back. Mr. Sticky went through the vampire's sternum like it was butter. Switch hands. Pull out the heart. Vampire dust. It was never very messy because their blood is thick and molasses dark. It tastes like moldy fruit. Don't ask me how I know that.

There was just enough time for me to duck into a shadow before I turned back to Kristen.

I carried the heart out to the parking lot, dropping it in a swing-top trashcan in front of McDonalds. One hand was slimed with vampire blood, and I kept wiping it on the hem of my cotton blouse long after it looked clean. All that and I still managed to make my bus.

The second tag was harder. My bus stop is in front of Safeway, about a quarter mile from my apartment complex down a two-lane road. Between the Safeway and my apartment there's a strip mall and a couple of old houses that have been turned into a hair salon and an insurance office then a soccer field that's ringed by trees. Most nights there are games going on, and the big field lights make walking that stretch like walking in the mall.

This was one of the off nights. When that patch of road is dark, it's really dark, so I scurried along, trying to get past it as quick as I could. At times like this times I could really tell the difference between myself and Jai. She attacks the dark patches like a panther in high-heeled boots, while I scamper across like a field mouse in sneakers. It's not something I'm proud of, but there you go. When I was almost past the dark soccer fields, something blasted into me, knocking me onto all fours in the gravel shoulder at the side of the road. I got a wave of nasty dead-critter smell. Vampire. One of the wild ones. The smell brought out Jai.

I stood up, brushing chips of rock off the heels of my hands. I wore jeans and a sweatshirt. Not my usual standard, but hey, this wasn't my usual tag. Mr. Sticky in hand, I turned to face the thing crouched in the grass about eight feet away from me. Its matted hair hung down around a face that was locked in a snarl. Its shredded clothes barely covered its body. Hard to tell whether it was a boy or a girl. It sprang at me again. I mostly dodged it, except where its claws caught one sleeve, tearing a gash that let my elbow show through.

Should have gone with a tank top.

It circled around, trying to find an angle that didn't involve Mr. Sticky. I'd met a couple of these wild ones before. Couldn't remember if there had always been wild vampires, or if this was a modern invention. Like other vamps, they couldn't leave me alone. Unlike other vamps, they seemed immune to my charms. Darn. The wild one came at me again, harder, windmilling its arms, frantic to get at my neck.

Mr. Sticky slipped in underneath. And that was that. Vampire dust.

Two days later I was in the store with Robbie. She worked the sales floor twice a week so I didn't have to be there from opening to closing every day, and she also took care of processing the on-line sales. Even *with* her help, I managed to find reasons to go to work six and a half days a week. I loved it. I also didn't have much else to do.

My bookstore, Reader's Corner, was in the Evergreen City Mall, a small complex northeast of Seattle that sits off a bend in Highway 522. It's one of the new-concept outdoor malls that were supposed to look like old fashioned town shopping districts, with lots of open air and landscaping that changed with every season. I could just afford the rent. Despite the general pummeling most independent bookstores were experiencing, my mix of used and new books and on-line sales was keeping the doors open. Barely.

Robbie ran our website from the office at the back of the store. There was a small desk and computer pushed up against one wall. Bookshelves lined the other three walls, mostly holding the used books that were listed on the website, on Amazon, and on eBay. The days when I worked alone, the office was tidy. When Robbie worked it was...not. Anything important, like papers that needed my signature, she stacked on the corner of the desk under a flat black rock that we'd found in an odd corner. No matter how much chaos she created in the rest of the office, she knew to keep my stack in its place under the rock.

So far I'd kept her in the dark about Jai. It wasn't hard. I'd never had much social life before Herbert bit me. Now I was out catching vampires in the evenings instead of sitting at home reading. Since neither activity lent itself to telling tales the day after, Robbie didn't notice the difference.

She was tidying up behind the counter and I was in the back of the store, kneeling on the floor, taking inventory of the books on the bottom shelf of the science section, when

Vivienne came in for a visit right about mid-morning. I saw her looking around, so I scuttled backwards, a pudgy crab in a denim skirt and espadrilles. I was aiming to get behind an end-cap display of the new cookbook, *100 Things to Do With Twinkies, Cream Cheese, and a Deep Fat Fryer*, by Paula Dean. Vivienne was quicker. Before I got two feet, she was staring down at me, probably getting an eyeful of what should have been under my skirt.

A light blue empire-waist dress fell loosely around her body, making her auburn hair look warmer than usual. She also wore a thick padded neck brace.

"Vivienne, you're…" I started to speak then stopped to tuck my legs under me so I was kneeling again. No more free show.

She smiled down at me with frigid eyes. "I'm feeling well, thank you."

"I thought you were, like, dead."

"Oh, that's the second or third time he's tried to take my head off in the last two hundred years."

"Wow, really? You must be a Renfield or something."

Her smile dropped away. "Don't be rude."

"Sorry." All I knew about vampires was how to kill them.

She shrugged then grimaced as if the movement had hurt her. "My Master sent me with a warning. You must stop being Jai's hostess. It's too dangerous."

"Um…No."

"He says you must. Jai's enemies have noted your activity."

At this point I noticed Herbert had come out from the back room and Robbie was leaning on the counter, staring at us with her mouth flopped open like a guppy. So much for my secret.

"What, she's not a vampire favorite? *Qu'elle* surprise."

Vivienne crossed her arms, looking prim and a little crazy. "If Jai dies, you die."

"Well thanks, Viv. You can tell your vampire friend that I'm properly warned."

"You are bringing ignorance and obstinacy to a dangerous situation."

"Yep, and Mr. Sticky."

"There are many ways to die." She turned and drifted out of the store.

I stayed where I was, hugging myself. I didn't dare turn around to see if Robbie had managed to close her mouth.

"So is this some kind of new RP you have going?" Robbie said to the side of my head. An RP, or role-play game, was the kind of thing we'd pretty much outgrown in college.

"Kristen," Herbert said.

He was heading in the direction of the counter, and Robbie looked around to see where the voice had come from. I was so screwed. Oops. Points off for me for using a naughty word.

"Not exactly," I answered.

She was giving me her puzzled look, pulling her brows together and looking at me down the end of her pointed nose. Herbert went right up the side of the counter, stopping about a foot from Robbie's elbow. Robbie wasn't supposed to know about any of this. In about two minutes she was going see Herbert and one thing was going to lead to the next. If I was lucky I might convince her Vivienne was a crazy person. A talking spider was harder to explain away.

When she saw Herbert she screamed loud enough to draw the attention of the shoppers out in the mall. Fortunately, the sound dissipated quickly in the open air beyond our roofline. People went back to their shopping when there was no other sign of drama.

"Shh, Rob, it's ok," I said, hurrying to stand next to her.

"Um, Kristen, there's a spider the size of a Chihuahua on the counter."

"I know. It's Herbert. He's kind of a pet."

"Pet?" he said, indignant.

Robbie screamed again. I grabbed her hands.

"You have to stop screaming or they'll send security in here." I wanted to get this over with before any customers showed up.

"Okay, okay, okay," she squeaked.

"Not a pet then. A friend."

"I might be going crazy," she said.

"No, see, it's like this," I started, and in the next ten minutes gave Robbie the *Cliff Notes* version of the last nine months of my life, the bite, and the change to Jai and Mr. Sticky, and vamp dust, and all.

"That's...wow..." she said when I was finished.

"That about sums it up," I said.

"Can we talk about your vamp friend and his freaky sidekick yet?" Herbert said.

We ignored him.

"So Mr. Sticky is magic or something." Robbie's face still had a squint-eyed, confused look. I gave her points for trying.

"It's a Dionysian brass blade, forged before Christ got strung up," Herbert said.

"Nailed up," I corrected.

"Whatever," Herbert continued. "It's three thousand years old and it was made to kill vampires. It comes with being Jai."

Robbie looked at me like I'd grown a second head. "You change into a whole different person."

Although we'd been best friends since high school, she was always the daring one. She was tall and lean. I wasn't. Her eyes were a bright clear blue. Mine were almost grey. She had the lead role in the school play, while I painted scenery and wrangled props. She'd had the first kiss, the first lover, the first husband. I'd been two steps from a virgin till Herbert bit me, since there wasn't much action for a bespectacled bookworm with soft white thighs. As Jai I sometimes had to get physical with the older and stronger vamps. If I couldn't distract them with a kiss or a nibble or some well-placed sucking, riding them to a climax made their brains squirt out their ears. That kept them distracted while Mr. Sticky went to work. I still loved a good book on a quiet evening, but being Jai was a whole lot of fun, too.

"I hope you never see Jai," I said honestly, squeezing her close.

"Enough warm fuzzy. We need a plan. Tell me again about this vampire." Herbert's eyes sparkled in the fluorescent lights.

"He was easily the oldest vamp I've ever encountered," I said, describing what he looked like, felt like, smelled like.

"He didn't touch you."

"It was like his arms turned to rocks."

"And his lair was near your house."

"Walking distance, actually. I stopped at Dick's on the way home."

Dick's Drive-In was next door to the Safeway on the Bothell-Everett Highway, about a quarter mile from my house. It was an old-fashioned kind of place, one where you walked up to the window, placed your order, then stood shivering under the overhanging roof until your food was ready. The Dick's Deluxe burger was an institution and the fries were legendary. I loved it.

"Too close," he said.

"You should come stay with me," Robbie said, jumping into the swing of things.

"He seemed more scared of me than I was of him."

"Yeah, this time you caught him off-guard," Herbert said. "It'll be different when he's had time to plan. You could end up dead."

"Nah." I was afraid to tell Herbert about the gold thread. It would take more evidence before I'd believe the few rules I knew had changed.

"Don't fool with this, Kristen. Jai and I have been together nearly as long as the sword has existed, and only once before has a vampire come close to killing her."

"And don't you go looking for the bogeyman. Vampires don't scare Jai, so they don't scare me."

He might have looked worried. It was hard to tell with a spider "Then you're both idiots."

CHAPTER 3

I stared out the window of the bus, thinking about what it meant to have Robbie in on my secret. It helped that Herbert was there when she found out. If I'd tried to tell her while we were out for a beer or something, she would have thought I was crazy, but it's hard to argue with a talking spider. It was Robbie's night to close the store and I could imagine her jumping at every shadow, tortured by the thought that Herbert was going to suddenly appear. Hopefully, there would be plenty of customers to keep her occupied.

The bus trip between the Evergreen City Mall and my apartment took about twenty-five minutes. I didn't drive much, choosing to take the bus to work to save the gas money. Just because the bookstore was making it didn't mean I could afford over three dollars a gallon for gas. Besides, I could always stop at Dick's if I didn't feel like cooking. It was all pretty convenient.

When it rained, I drove to the Safeway and left my car in the lot. I considered it my own personal Park & Ride. Today, there was no rain as I walked home, though a high overcast muted the incipient sunset.

I lived far enough off the highway that I couldn't hear the street noise, with the added bonus that I could classify the walks to and from the bus as actual exercise. I didn't push the walking thing, though.

Home was a two-bedroom apartment in a woodsy, nineteen-seventies complex at the edge of a subdivision. In addition to the two bedrooms, I had a too-small kitchen and a little balcony that looked out over the parking lot. The building was surrounded by tall evergreens, and if I didn't look down I could sit out on the balcony and fool myself into thinking I lived in a forest.

As soon as I let myself into the apartment, my cat Petunia started scolding me with loud, yodeling mews.

"As if you ever do more than sleep all day." I scolded back. She was a cream-colored Siamese with grey points, one wrinkled ear and the stub of a tail. Something bad had happened to her before I found her at the kitty halfway house. She wouldn't tell me what it was. She leaped up on the arm of the couch so I could scratch the top of her head on my way by. "Let's go out on the balcony and check out the 'hood.'"

She followed me out. I leaned my elbows on the rough cedar railing, and she jumped up next to me, chattering at the birds and switching her tail back and forth.

I was worried about Robbie. After all, I'd had nine months to get used to the idea of a talking spider. It hadn't been easy. The first few days I was sure I was going crazy, and the first time I shifted into Jai on my own, I thought my head would explode. When that first vampire was dead and

Jai faded away, I stood there holding a gooey heart with a pile of black dust at my feet and thought I must have had some kind of psychotic breakdown. But it kept happening once or twice a week. After a month or so, when everything else stayed the same, I relaxed.

It got to be fun.

Before Herbert and Jai, I had only a few friends, the store, and my books. Without Jai I was all tough talk and shadowboxing. I could trade one-liners with the best of them, but Mom always told me that sarcasm was the weapon of the weak. Inside I was the consistency of baby food, so scared of life I worried I'd never really live.

"I bet if you saw a talking spider, you would freak out, too." I said to Petunia.

She ignored me, concentrating on the parking strip where one of my neighbors was tossing a ball to her Scots Terrier. Petunia was queen of the balcony and she lorded it over those lesser beings who crawled on the earth.

"A dog would pay more attention to me, you know."

I shook my head and walked back into the apartment, leaving Petunia to hold court. I wasn't too worried that she'd jump off the balcony. We were three floors up, and if she did, she'd get what she deserved. That Scots Terrier looked like the type to hold a grudge.

As I fished through the refrigerator for some inspiration, I debated whether I should go on a vampire hunt. Herbert had given me a small glass vial of vampire essence that hung on a thin gold chain. Wearing it brought Jai out so I could go looking for vamps. A couple times a week I'd head out to clubs where vampires were likely to hang out, looking for victims. But Herbert's warning made me cautious.

The freezer gave up a packet of frozen scallops that begged to be sautéed with garlic and tossed with a little parmesan. I boiled some water then poured too much pasta in, rationalizing that I could take the leftovers to work for lunch. If there were any leftovers. The scallops were precooked and just needed to be thawed before they joined the sweating garlic in the pan of hot olive oil.

It was all coming together so nicely when something cracked against the sliding glass door. Petunia came screaming in from the balcony, her fur spread out twice its normal size.

"Holy shizzle."

I walked slowly towards the door to the balcony. It was about eight p.m. The sky was dim because of the overcast , so I turned on the balcony light. There was a smear of brown in the middle of the sliding glass door. Something small and dark lay on the green indoor-outdoor carpet that covered the balcony floor. I bent slowly toward it.

It was a rat. A dead rat. The parking lot was empty, and I didn't see anyone standing in the trees. No whiff of vampire stink. I left it on the balcony and slipped back inside, closing and locking the door behind me. The scallops burned and the pasta got boggy while I stood staring out into the trees, arms wrapped around myself. After a while the only light was a little halo from the bulb next to my sliding glass door, so I pulled the drapes shut then opened them again. I felt more vulnerable when I couldn't see what might be out there or who it was that threw a dead rat up three floors.

After warnings from Vivienne and Herbert both, I never entertained the thought the thing might have landed on my balcony by mistake. I had no one to call, no roommate to keep me company, no one to help. Robbie was too new to all this and Herbert was, well, a spider. I scraped dinner into the trash and opened a beer. Jai would be staying home. I was suddenly in the mood for the company of old friends like Harry, Ron, and Hermione, or maybe for a trip to Earthsea.

I came into work at lunchtime to take over the register so Robbie could go in the back and process on-line orders. She was covering the morning shift. Two days had passed since she'd met Herbert and learned about Jai.

"Herbert was skulking around," Robbie said.

I handed her the spicy chicken burrito from World Wrapps that I'd brought her for lunch. "Hmph. Sometimes I don't see him for days."

"Did it hurt when he bit you?" She had been pretending to tidy up the bestseller rack, front and center between the door to the mall and the register. I knew she was really just reading the jackets to see which ones she wanted to buy.

"The bite felt like any spider bite would." I was such a set-up for Herbert, it still made me shake my head. "He caught me as I was walking home from the bus after working all day. It had started to rain, so I was hurrying, and almost didn't notice him at first. The weird thing was when he started to talk."

"Yeah, that totally freaked me out."

"A sensible person might have run screaming." I shrugged. "You know how I feel about running. My feet hurt and I was tired. I let him crawl into my bag and carried him home. He explained the situation while I drank a glass of wine or two, and then I let him bite me."

"I can't believe he talked you into it."

I shrugged again. "It was all one big romantic adventure. At least I thought it was. Take that in the back if a customer comes in," I said as Robbie peeled the foil from one end of her burrito and leaned her elbows on the counter.

"Yes, boss."

"Oh hush." I shot her a dirty look. "The first time I changed was, well, more than I expected. I mean, he'd said Jai was tall and beautiful. Having it actually happen to me was seriously cool." I gulped and my cheeks started to flame. It was hard to explain how it felt to go from short and dumpy to va-va-voom in the space of three heartbeats.

"The other day you said you hoped I'd never meet Jai." Robbie took a careful bite of her wrap. She knew I'd complain if she spilled on the counter. I'm fussy that way.

"I only turn into Jai if there's a vampire around. They're not the best company."

"Okay, yeah, about the whole vampire thing?"

"Don't think about it too hard."

"So Buffy and Twilight are true?"

"Most authors get parts of the story, well, except maybe the bit in Twilight about the sparkles." I stared out through the store windows as if I would see vampires striding through the middle of the mall. That was unlikely, since the sun was shining and it would turn them to dust in about three minutes. "The part about them frying in the sun is true."

Four teenage girls came into the store clutching bags from The Gap and Vans Shoes.

"I'm gone," Robbie said, grabbing her wrap and ducking into the back office.

After they left, taking copies of *Clockwork Angel* and *The Hunger Games* with them, I went to check on her.

"C'mere, I want you to see something," Robbie said when she saw me. She was sitting at the computer looking at the photo of a smiling thirty-something man, the kind of guy who shaved his head to hide the receding hairline.

"Who's that?"

"I just registered you on Match.com. He's one of your hits. The thing is I think he works in the same group as Doug." Robbie's husband was a Microsoft employee for the last fifteen years. He'd written code for every version of Windows since Win95, and I was pretty sure Robbie was the only woman he knew who didn't speak Tetrus or Orca or whatever the latest computer language was.

"He looks, um, nice, I guess."

"And he's a real guy. Like, he can go out in the sun and you won't have to kill him."

"Those are definite plusses."

She smiled. "I'm going to have Doug ping him."

I shrugged. Given what I knew of Doug's social skills, I wasn't overly worried. There hadn't been a guy since high school who'd come close to meeting my expectations. Robbie said I read too many books.

Whatever.

She was tapping away at the keyboard when I went back out into the store.

CHAPTER 4

John, you must feed," Vivienne said, rising from the daybed where she'd been awaiting sunset.

"I hate this time of year," he said. He paused just inside the doorway. "The daylight never ends."

Vivienne heard the rough edge to his voice. "You need blood."

"Not yours, Little Bird. You have only recently recovered your strength. I cannot steal from it so soon."

"John."

She moved toward him in a liquid swirl of diaphanous gown, the hem barely kissing her bare feet. Raising her arm, she offering her wrist.

His fingers wrapped around hers, lowering her hand to rest against her breast. "Nay, Little Bird."

"You're going to her, aren't you? That's why you won't feed," she said and rested her forehead on his chest, her arms twining around him.

"I'm going out to find someone who's willing to donate, yes. It's only truly dark for about forty five minutes at this time of year, so you would be wise not to delay me," he said. His grin showed that he was only pretending to scold her.

She took a step back from him and pushed out her lower lip, teasing him back. "Just any old donor?"

"Tread carefully, Vivienne."

"She nearly ended you."

"Is it only me you worry about?" he asked. "If I die, so do you."

She ignored the thread of sarcasm in his words. "Let us leave here. We'll go someplace where the sun sets earlier in the day."

"Don't," he said, running his fingertips along the side of her throat. "Rest, Little Bird. I shall return before morning." He pulled her knuckles to his lips before turning to go.

"John, please..."

"Rest. Allow yourself to heal."

It was a fairly quiet day. Robbie left at five to go home and try to make a baby. She might get lucky, although Doug worked typical Microsoft hours, which didn't always allow for much of a life outside work. Closing was at nine so it was nearly dark when I left the store. Halfway to the bus I smelled him. I knew it was Shakespeare. From one step to the next I was Jai. My white cotton capris and camp shirt had become a bright fuchsia mini dress and sky-high black pumps. My fuzzy French braid was now a gentle cascade of brown, parted so it fell in a swoosh across my face, hiding one eye.

"Come out, come out, Shakespeare." The straps that held Mr. Sticky's sheath pinched my bare thigh. Around me, the parking lot was nearly empty of cars, just a grid of white stripes on the expanse of black pavement.

"The days and months and years turn, and still your beauty holds my heart." He was behind me, his cold fingers moving my hair aside so he could trace the line of my neck.

"You must be feeling lucky...or brave," I said.

"And you are in danger. The Queen is seeking you."

"What Queen? This is America." I leaned back into his body and grinned when he stiffened against my curves.

"Think, Jai," he said into my hair. His fingertips brushed my cheek. I spun around to face him, feeling my skirt ride up as I moved. "The Vampire Queen. You have battled her before."

"Have I battled you before, too?"

"Nay, I have been drawn to you for lifetimes." The smile he gave me held all kinds of promise. "The Queen is more powerful than any other vampire, the only one among us who has the strength to make new vamps. She has no love for one who destroys them."

"Makes sense."

"She has threatened to destroy both of us, though for different reasons." He leaned closer to me, our lips nearly touching. I slipped Mr. Sticky out of its sheath. "Put your toy away. You'll not use it on me." And he kissed me.

He was right.

Vampire kisses usually only lasted as long as it took for me to slice open their chest. This was different. He held my upper arms lightly but his mouth was demanding, hungry, forcing me to kiss him back. Mr. Sticky dropped to the pavement. On their own my hands grasped his waist. Wow. Kissing could be more fun than I realized.

"I didn't kill you," I said after several long minutes.

"And you won't so long as I keep you well distracted." He grinned at me, looking younger and softer. From up close the thread of goodness was easier to see.

"Stupid vampire," I whispered, mightily pissed off all of a sudden. It was easier to be angry than scared. I pushed away from him.

"Too long you've been alone. I fear you truly do not remember." His smile dimmed, then he looked sharply over my shoulder. "Pick up your blade. The Queen comes."

I stepped away from him and grabbed Mr. Sticky.

The Queen had been carved from alabaster and rose. She came round the corner past the big Anthropologie store that anchored the north end of the mall, strolling arm in arm with two pretty young boys. Her hair was a heavy strawberry blond bob, her skin was perfectly white with just the hint of a blush, and she wore a cream-colored dropped-waist gown with a deep pink ribbon as a belt. It had probably been the height of fashion in nineteen twenty-five.

"Two naughty children sitting in a tree, K-I-S-S-I-N-G," she murmured when she got close to us.

"My Lady." Shakespeare bowed his head. I didn't.

"Sir John." She extended her hand to him, nodding once as he bent to kiss it.

I crossed my arms, flicking the hair out of my eyes with a shake. Vampire Queen. I snorted. Whatever.

"And you." She turned to me. "The dreadnought, the immortal one, the killer. I thought you'd be....classier." Her eyes raked my body. She didn't offer to let me kiss her hand.

"And I thought you'd be scarier," I said, though that was a lie. Up close, her power was like the glare from the setting sun on a wet freeway. I couldn't look away despite how bad it hurt my eyes.

"You are correct, Lady Merliadne. This is Jai." Shakespeare said. Apparently his real name was Sir John. He could have told me.

She gave me a frosty glance and turned back to him. "Someone has been trying to make vampires, Sir John, but they're not doing a good job of it."

"You have found feral vampires, Lady Merliadne?"

"I've destroyed several," she said, loosening her grip on the young vamps standing next to her and moving towards him. "You're the only one around old enough to even try."

"By my word, I have not, My Lady."

She stared up at him, eyes wide and black, as if trying to see past his surface. What she saw made her purse her pretty lips. "If not you, then who? Tell me why I shouldn't kill you both, Sir John, especially this one."

Ooh, bummer. She remembered I was there. Shakespeare wrapped his arm around my waist, pulling me close. "Do you want to destroy her, My Lady, or make use of her?"

"I'm not sure I have use for either of you."

"Really? You didn't think that in Paris." He smiled at her, giving her a full dose of his testosterone-fueled confidence. Ballsy strategy, what with my blade so close and the taste of his tongue all fresh in my mouth.

"Paris was a long time ago. Reminding me of it makes me want to kill you twice."

"If you kill me, then you've lost an ally and a friend. If you kill her, you lose a weapon. She would help you destroy the feral vampires while we look for their maker."

"She won't fight for me. That demon who keeps her will see to that."

"Hey, can the chopped liver you're arguing over get a word in?"

Now I was back on the angry train. I pulled away from Shakespeare. The move put me closer to one of her companions. He was slender and looked maybe twenty-two years old, all Goth'ed out in black with enough guy-liner to cover the city. His head turned toward me as if he'd just caught my scent. He smiled, his fangs pressing into his lower lip, and dropped the Queen's arm.

"Damien, get back here," she snarled as he came towards me. He caught me up in his arms and started rubbing his face against my hair. Growling and purring, having a great time. Too bad Mr. Sticky was already in my hand.

Over the baby vamp's head I could see Shakespeare watching the Queen. She didn't look all that concerned. Oh well. I went to work, and a few seconds later I was standing there with the vamp's heart in my hand and a pile of dust at my feet. The gooey squish of his heart between my fingers took the edge off my anger. I pointed Mr. Sticky at the Queen.

"Maybe you're not immune to me, either," I said, taking a step towards her.

That got Shakespeare's attention, and he thrust himself between us, even as the other boy started to move. Shakespeare caught him on his way by.

"My Lady, coming here with only these youngsters seems ill-advised."

"Let me have him, Shakespeare," I said with a nasty glare. "He'll die with a smile on his face."

"My name is Sir John Robartes, Earl of Radnor. Now please hold your tongue." The look he gave me put an exclamation point on his words. As if he could really scare me.

"C'mon, Shakespeare, let me kill the baby vamp."

I reached out towards him. The young one wrestled with Shakespeare. His thick blond dreadlocks were tied back with a patterned scarf and the angular tailoring of his black tunic and slacks looked like it had come straight from the runway of a Japanese fashion show.

"Let him go, Sir John," the Queen said so softly I wasn't sure I heard it.

Then Dreadlocks was pulling me in for a kiss. Mr. Sticky got in the way. Oops. There'd be two hearts for the McDonald's trashcan tonight.

"It's what the modern people call, 'collateral damage,'" she said as I dropped the second heart at my feet with the first one.

The three of us stood silent for a moment.

"You make a compelling argument, John." The Queen grinned, as inappropriate a look as a smile on a wildcat. "Do you think you can keep her in line like before?"

"I can and I will," Shakespeare said.

I alternated between pointing Mr. Sticky at the Queen and pointing it at Shakespeare.

"I will consider your request." She did one of those vampire things and was gone before I could blink.

"We have a reprieve," Shakespeare said.

"I'm still gonna call you Shakespeare."

After the Queen left, Shakespeare wanted to pick up where we left off. The idea had its appeal, but I had vampire blood smeared across my cute pink dress and an uneasy feeling, as if I should know more about this situation than I did. I sent him off to do vampire things, and as soon as his pungent smell faded, I morphed back into Kristen, fuzzy ponytail, capris, camp shirt, and all.

☠

At that time of night, the bus schedule was more of a suggestion, so I had no idea how long the wait would be. Usually that wouldn't bug me, and I'd have been happy to spend the time reading or just daydreaming. That night all I wanted was home.

Petunia picked up on my disquiet, jumping up into my lap as soon as I slumped against the back of the couch. She went to work kneading my belly through the baggy sweatpants I'd changed into, while I sipped a beer and stared out the sliding glass door into the trees. How had my life gotten so out of control? If my soul had a mirror, I would have seen the real problem was that Jai wanted Shakespeare. She wanted him in a very specific, physical way. As usual, I wanted to skip ahead and read the ending. I was two-thirds of the way through my beer when something thumped onto my balcony. I was so not in the mood for another dead rat.

It was a string of garlic cloves. I was standing there fingering their smooth sides—someone had taken the time to peel them—when a familiar rich voice came up from the darkness below.

"Lady Kristen, if you please, put it on like a necklace."

I draped the garlic around my shoulders, twisting the two end cloves together to join the circle, and closed the sliding glass door. A moment later a dark figure leapt onto my balcony and knocked on the aluminum doorframe.

I opened it slowly. "You could have come through the front door like everyone else."

Shakespeare stood just outside the glass. "If it pleases My Lady, invite me in."

"So this was just quicker, I guess."

"Please."

"And the garlic is for…"

"So I can talk with Kristen without Jai's appearance."

"I'm not tough when I'm Kristen. You could hurt me."

"On my honor, lady. I am here to do you no harm."

"I think that's a double negative, but come in anyway." I stood back so Shakespeare could step into the apartment.

Petunia jumped up on the arm of the couch and stared at him. She had her mouth open in that "I'm huffing your scent to get to know you" way that cats have. In less than a minute she squawked and took off down the hall. She's not much of a guard cat.

He made his way around my room, examining my bookshelves and fingering the tchotkes I had laying around. I liked my living room. There was the couch and a big comfortable chair, and the walls were lined with bookcases. Stacks of thick reference books and glossy photo books served in place of end-tables.

Shakespeare was dressed simply in a black long-sleeved tee-shirt tucked into Levis. A vampire in Levis. Huh. His shoulders were broader than I'd noticed before and they narrowed easily to slim hips. It was a swimmer's body, long and lean. I plunked myself gracelessly on the edge of the couch and watched him move around.

"You are a great reader," he said.

"It goes with owning a bookstore."

He abruptly turned to face me. "I assure you that Vivienne did not know you were Jai."

"I could tell. I thought your eyes were going to pop out of your head when Jai got up off that bed."

"This ring offers me protection from Jai's power." There was a gold band studded with three green stones on the fourth finger of his left hand.

"You weren't wearing it the other night."

"No. I'll not make that mistake again. Vivienne and I heard rumors that something in this area was destroying vampires, so we came here looking for Jai. We've been searching for her for so long, you see."

"You found her."

"Yes, in a most unexpected way."

"So why did Vivienne grab me?"

"The nights are short at this time of year, and we had not found Jai. I was....what you'd call, depressed, I think."

Okay, knock me over with a feather. Levis and depression. *So* not what I expected from a vampire.

"There is something I need to know." He came closer to me. "Are you happy with your role as Jai's hostess?"

"Happy? Well, yeah."

"Perhaps you are ready to return to your own life."

"No." I jumped up. The thought of going back to my boring old life was horrifying. "I like Jai. I have fun with her."

"By my word, your experience has been truncated."

He turned his back to me and stared out the sliding glass door. I could see his fists clenching.

"Feels full enough to me."

"Jai and I shared a life for many years. We worked together to kill only those vampires who deserved it, until the one who hates me nearly destroyed us both. I was forced to retire from the world for a time, to regain my strength, and since I returned, the demon has kept Jai hidden, moving her frequently between hostesses and limiting her activity."

"I don't know any demons." I stared out the window over his shoulder.

"You must. He's Jai's guardian, a temporal demon."

"Herbert's a spider, not a demon."

"Ah, he is calling himself Herbert again." He pronounced it 'Hair-bairt'. "The spider is only one of his forms."

"I guess I knew the talking spider thing was too strange to be the whole story."

"We could have it again," he said, then turned away from me and balled up one fist, as if he regretted his own words. "We could fight for the Queen, find the one who's making the ferals."

I leaned forward, resting my elbows on my knees. "Do what now, exactly?"

"Nothing. My apologies, My Lady." Shakespeare turned back to me and smiled, although there was pain in his eyes. "You are lovely, Lady Kristen. Your eyes are as delicate as raindrops and your smile is warmer than the sun."

"Thanks, um, I guess. Can I get you something? I need another beer." I picked my bottle up and downed the last swallow.

Clearly I didn't have Jai's immunity to his charm. The thought of what might be hiding under those Levi's made my head spin.

"No, thank you. I already had something to drink."

Okay, didn't want to think about that too hard. I left him standing in the living room while I went to the refrigerator. I opened the beer, took a swallow, then pulled off the garlic. I didn't plan it, didn't want to consider the implications. Right then, Jai was driving our bus.

CHAPTER 5

I wore the same baggy sweatpants that Kristen had put on after work. The waist was too big, so they road low on my hips. Despite that they were still several inches too short. Instead of a sloppy sweatshirt, I had on a tight white men's undershirt tied in a knot right above my belly button. I'd also somehow lost my bra. Oh well. When I walked in Shakespeare looked like he'd been shot.

"Dude, have some class," I said. Shakespeare just stared. "Come on, don't go zombie on me."

"Jai, I..."

"You got nothing to say, then." I crossed the room to stand arm's length from him.

He reached for me and I closed the gap between us.

"You are my one true love." He leaned over and kissed me.

"I wish I could remember why," I said under his lips.

It was a long time before either of us spoke again. Shakespeare's hands found their way around my body with a familiarity I'd never experienced before. He knew just where to touch, how fast, how hard. I was slower, discovering the muscular plains of his chest, over his shoulders, across his back. Whoa. When he pushed me down on the couch and straddled me, I met his eyes.

"John," I whispered.

He smiled, his eyes heavy with an emotion I didn't recognize. "That's better than Shakespeare."

"The first thing I ever heard you say sounded like it came from one of his plays." I reached up and pulled his face towards me so I could lick his bottom lip, fascinated with its taste and texture.

From this close, I didn't notice his pungent vampire smell. He kissed me more slowly, letting me get to know the feel of his skin, the roughness of the stubble he hadn't shaved away. His hands were working their way up under my tee-shirt. He pressed himself against me and when I felt the full hard length of him it dawned on me that unless I flashed a red light right now, we were going to have sex. I knew somehow that Kristen had had drunken sex once with a boy she knew in college. A couple of times I'd done it as a warm-up to a kill. Not exactly an extensive resume, but enough to recognize the road we were on.

I pulled away.

"What is it, Jai?"

"Listen, you can't just come in here and paw me like I'm some kind of slut."

"Forgive me." Shakespeare stood up slowly, pulling me to my feet. "By my word, I would have you remember what we shared, my love." He kept his arms around me but gave me a little space.

I needed it. "I thought all vampires were evil, but you're not. I can see goodness in you."

"All vampires are different, as all humans are different. The demon has taught you that we all deserve to die, and maybe he is correct. We all prey on humans. But demons and vampires are natural enemies, so he has, perhaps, a bias."

"Maybe not all of you deserve to die."

"You knew that once. We worked together to apply your gifts only where they were needed."

It was a struggle, but I pulled my brain together to consider what he said. "That could work."

"Yes." He bent to kiss me again.

"You were with her," Vivienne said. She was draped across his big brass bed, the hem of her lace gown torn and tangled around her legs. Only one candle still gave any light. The rest had burned low.

"Little Bird, you should be asleep."

"Don't be kind to me. You're going to go off again, and I can't bear it."

"Be reasonable, Vivienne. You are tied to me in a way that no other woman is."

"Reasonable? Fie." She sprang to her feet, swaying slightly. "Down here in the dark waiting, always waiting. You come and feed…and leave. After all this time, you leave me."

"Vivienne," he said.

She hated the compassion in his voice. "No, not again. I'm going this time." She took two steps towards the door, feeling a little steadier on her feet.

"It has always been your choice to stay or not."

"Then I'm…." She ran out of the room, her voice muffled by tears. She could tell he wasn't coming after her. They both knew she couldn't survive without him. A poisonous cocktail of anger and shame flooded her as she searched for a place to hide, at least until the sun rose.

I took two cold showers after he left, which was okay at the time. I really didn't feel tired until the alarm went off in the morning. Scraping myself out of bed, I drove to the bus stop, too lazy to walk. I also managed to wake up in time to get off the bus at the right stop. When I let myself into the store, though, I found something that woke me up faster than any cup of coffee.

There was a large black spider in a pool of blood near the cash register. It wasn't directly on the counter; someone had stacked up books into what looked like an altar, and the spider was lying on top. Blood pooled and dripped down the books. I stumbled across the store, thinking that Herbert had met an untimely end. When I got closer I could see that it was a stuffed spider, and the red liquid was ketchup. All the books that had been used for the altar were about vampires.

"Herbert," I screamed. "Come out here now."

Silence. Then I heard a tapping sound coming from the back of the store. I opened the office door slowly, and heard it again.

"Herbert?"

"Damn, girl, open the drawer." The voice was muffled and the tapping seemed to be coming from the top drawer in the file cabinet. I pulled it open and Herbert glared up at me. The files had been pushed towards the back so that there was just enough space for him, though his legs looked pretty cramped. When the drawer was open far enough, he popped out. I didn't remember till later to speak to him about his use of bad language.

"Don't even ask how I got in there. It seemed like a good idea at the time," he said.

I opened my mouth to speak then closed it. Opened it again. And closed it again. "I'm just glad you're alive."

Together we walked out into the store to look at the mess on the counter.

"I should call the police," I said.

"Nah, it was a vampire."

"Insurance won't pay for any damage unless there's a police report."

"Call them then, but they won't find anything. He was just trying to scare you."

"He? Who?"

"Would you believe me if I told you it was a tall handsome vampire with short golden curls?"

"Shakespeare?"

"I'm just sayin'."

"No, he wouldn't do this. He couldn't have. He was, um, busy."

It felt like there was a band around my head with a matching one around my heart. They both hurt. I was way too tired for this.

"It happened pretty early this morning."

"No. It wasn't him."

"Suit yourself." Herbert crawled up onto the counter next to his stuffed effigy.

"I should call Robbie, at least."

"That's better."

Robbie was there in an hour. With the exception of the one bare shelf in the Horror Section, I had the store looking like it was supposed to. The ketchup-stained books couldn't be sold as new, so I decided I'd wiped them down and set up a one dollar table near the register. From the register I could see the whole store; maybe not every book, but most of the places people were likely to stand and shop. When Robbie arrived I was planted behind the counter, reassuring myself that things were really all right.

Robbie came over straightaway and gave me a big hug. "I can't believe that someone messed this place up like that. You look like you want to cry."

"Nah, I'm okay, more or less." Liar. I did want to cry when I saw her.

Herbert was hidden but I could fell his sparkly black eyes on me, dissecting my response. The need to act tough in front of him helped me stay in control.

"I hope the cops find the guy."

"Didn't call them."

"Seriously?"

"Well, Herbert said it was a vampire, so I'll sell the books he ruined as used. No harm done."

Robbie moved out from behind the counter, staring at me like I'd lost my hold on reality. "Um, listen, it is hard to argue with the talking spider, and I guess I can get my brain around the vampire thing, but now you're heading into crazyland. Someone broke into your place. You call the cops when that happens."

"It wasn't that big a deal. A stuffed spider, a little ketchup, I mean, the dead rat last week was freakier."

"Dead rat?" Robbie put both hands on the counter very slowly.

"Oh. I guess I forgot to tell you about that."

"I guess you did."

I told her about someone throwing the rat at my sliding glass window and then spent another thirty minutes or so convincing her that nothing else weird had happened. Well, besides Vivienne grabbing me. Robbie was getting more and more worked up and anything I said made it worse.

"So you get drugged and kidnapped, then someone throws a dead rat on your balcony, and *then* someone pretends to kill your weird little spider friend." She had her arms crossed and nodded to emphasize each point.

"Did she mention that the vampire involved in the kidnapping looked a lot like the one who was here last night?" Herbert had popped out from wherever it was he hid.

"No, I didn't mention that." I turned to face him, giving him my best "shut up" look.

"And did she also tell you that this same vampire looks a lot like the one that almost killed Jai fifty years ago?"

"You were going to tell me that when? Besides, it wasn't him. I know it." I glared at both of them.

"You've got your head up your ass," he said

"And you're a rude little spider and don't swear at me." I was as close to angry as I ever got.

"If you don't like me, maybe I should take Jai and find a different hostess."

I scratched a hand through my ponytail, willing myself to calm down. "No...no, it's okay. Don't take Jai. You guys are blowing this up into something way bigger than it needs to be."

"Then listen when I tell you to be careful," Herbert said.

"Be careful," Robbie echoed him.

"Yes, of course. Kill vampires, don't kiss them. Oops." I covered my mouth with my hand.

"Kiss them," Robbie sounded more than surprised.

"If you go anyplace near that vampire again, I'm taking Jai." I'd never heard Herbert sound so serious.

"I have a plan for tonight." Robbie came into the office with a smirk on her face.

"If it doesn't involve sleeping, I'm not interested." I paused in the book order I was preparing, trying to rebuild the parts of the Horror Section that had been doused with ketchup. Shakespeare's late visit the night before was starting to really weigh me down.

"There'll be sleeping, just not right away."

"Don't keep me in suspense."

"Well, Doug is working till at least eight. And so is the rest of his team."

"Doug always works late, and presumably so does the rest of his team."

"Well, Corey does in fact work with Doug."

I rubbed my eyes behind my glasses, trying to remember if I knew anyone named Corey. "Help me out here. I'm drawing a blank."

Robbie leaned against the doorjamb and grinned at me. "Corey, the guy from Match.com. I showed you his picture last week."

Match.com—Match.com. "Yeah, um, he was bald, right?

"So what? Doug says he's a nice guy."

"And you think I should go out with him."

"They're meeting us here at nine-fifteen for pizza and beers at Romios."

"A date."

"A double-date. It'll be so much fun. I promise."

Robbie looked so hopeful that I couldn't say no. I wanted to though. I really wanted to. "Sure. If you stay out front, I'll get everything finished back here so we can be done by then."

She smiled, all blue eyes and fizzy energy. I did my best to smile back.

CHAPTER 6

Corey held the slice of pepperoni pizza poised halfway to his mouth. "So you think you make a good lasagna?"

Robbie laughed. "Oh no, she makes the best lasagna. Ever."

I shrugged. We were seated in a booth at Romios, a family restaurant stuck on the east end of the mall. There was an empty pitcher of microbrew-du-jour in front of us and another one on the way. Robbie and I were sitting on one side of the table and Corey and Doug were on the other.

"Anyone looking at me can see I like to cook," I said, smiling despite the fatigue and sloshing some beer on the honest-to-gosh red checked tablecloth in front of me.

"Gotta love a girl who knows her way around the kitchen." Corey grinned at me when I bristled. "I mean, that's not all she's good for, but still."

"Dude, you are so not scoring points." Robbie laughed again, which made me smile.

Corey caught my eye and almost winked. Maybe I was just too tired to come up with the list of faults I usually found when I met someone new. He was nice. I liked him.

"Hey girlfriend, let me out," I said during the next lull in conversation.

"I'll come with you," Robbie answered.

Going to the restroom together is a time-honored women's tradition. We crossed the busy restaurant, angling between the tables and dodging the occasional child-at-large.

Robbie looked at me tentatively as soon as the bathroom door swung shut. "So…"

"He makes me laugh. In a good way, I mean."

"Doug said he was totally into meeting you."

"Well, we'll have to see what he says now that he's met me." We took care of business and were washing hands side by side when Robbie stopped me.

"He's real, Kristen. He didn't come out of a book. Give him a chance."

I didn't know how to answer her.

After the pizza was finished and the second pitcher poured around the table, the conversation got a little sloppy. Corey was leaning towards me resting on his forearms, thumbs making little circles in the sweat on the side of his glass. Robbie and Doug were quietly making eyes at each other, probably playing footsie under the table.

"So you're not seeing anyone?" Corey asked me.

I had to think before I answered. "No, not really."

I mean, my superhero alter-ego was apparently involved with a vampire, or something , but there was no easy way to explain it.

"Well, I mean, I don't want to step on anybody's toes."

I sat up straighter. "No toes. No. I mean it."

Corey smiled into his glass. "Good."

His head was shaved nearly bald, with just a tonsure of fine reddish stubble. He was built like a grown-up high-school athlete. His shoulders were broad and I could see the bulge of his biceps, although his middle suggested he spent a lot of time behind a desk. That didn't bother me. My middle was nothing to write home about.

"What about you?"

"Single. Divorced, actually. Three years ago."

"Ouch."

"Old news. We got married right out of college. Too young, I guess."

"The divorce thing is never easy."

"Well, we didn't have kids, so that made it easier. She decided she wanted to be a writer when she grew up, so she moved down to California. I was blocking her dream."

"Too bad about *your* dreams."

"Well, it took a while before I had any interest in dating, that's for sure." He grinned at me again and I smiled back, feeling foolish and a little drunk. "I'm a lot more into it now."

"Hey, you two, get a room," Doug said, holding Robbie's hand across the tabletop.

"Don't be an asshole, Doug," Robbie said.

"And don't you swear," I scolded her.

"Sorry Mom." Robbie turned to Corey. "It's her pet peeve," she whispered.

"I'll remember that," Corey said, and we went back to smiling at each other.

At the end of the evening there was some good-natured arm-wrestling over who would pay the bill, then they all objected when I said I'd take the bus home. Robbie was especially upset by that. Corey politely insisted on driving me home, and after some halfhearted protests I gave in, though he had to move a couple ice axes and a heavy-duty pair of hiking boots off the passenger seat of his Nissan Xterra to make room for me.

"You really didn't have to do this," I said as we pulled south onto Highway 522.

"I wanted to. It gives me the chance to hang out with you some more." He caught my eye, headlights from the oncoming traffic making his face glow. Strangely, his interest seemed sincere.

We chatted happily about nothing till we got to my apartment. I didn't want to invite him in, although kissing him wasn't out of the question. "So, can I have your email address or a cell phone number or something?" he asked.

"Sure, I mean, of course."

He recorded it in his I-Phone after first making me promise not to tell anyone at Microsoft that he owned an Apple product. I just wrote *his* number down on an old receipt from the bottom of my purse. When I moved to get out of the car he reached for my hand, pulling it slowly toward his mouth, as if he was giving me time to escape. He kissed my knuckles gently then let me go.

"Good night, Kristen. I'll call you."

As I ran towards the building I held the hand he'd kissed against my chest. The kiss had been a surprisingly old-fashioned gesture. Just before I opened the front door I stopped. There it was, very faint, almost an echo rather than an actual scent. Vampire. Maybe Shakespeare. Then it was gone. I closed the door and hit the button for the elevator.

One week later I was at a loss. I was home from work with no real plans for the evening. Corey called every day or emailed me links to YouTube videos he thought would make me laugh. We even had plans for a Saturday night movie, which I was trying real hard not to think about. I was afraid I'd come up with too many reasons not to go.

In all that time, I hadn't seen a vampire. No Shakespeare, no crazy wild vamp that needed killing. I'd barely even seen Herbert. I could feel Jai pacing inside me—a really awkward sensation. With no vamps around I couldn't see a reason to let her out, and didn't feel like putting on the necklace with the vial of vampire essence. The pressure from her was building, but I wasn't in the mood.

I decided to make a frittata for dinner because it was quick. I used a couple of organic eggs, some sundried tomatoes from the jar in the fridge, minced garlic, and a fresh package of goat cheese. It was yummy. Afterwards I sat on the couch with Petunia in my lap and tried to decide if the missing vampires worried me.

The store had been busy and my feet were tired, so I was happy just to sit. I was too distracted to pick up anything from the stack of books in my T.B.R. pile on the floor. I got to thinking about the fact that Petunia was twelve or thirteen, an old lady in cat years. It made me sad to think that sometime soon she was going to die. She was such a presence, so vital, so close to the end. That must be how vampires feel about humans. We show up, tangle ourselves in the warp and weft of their lives, then die, leaving them to straighten out our messes. No wonder they'd rather kill us up front.

After a while I picked Petunia up and carried her across to the sliding glass window. I stared out into the trees then watched as the guy who lived down the hall from me pulled out of the parking lot in his vintage Mustang GT. Muscle head. When the car was gone I thought I saw movement just past the halo of light cast by the streetlamp. I stared into the dark, getting closer to the window so I wouldn't be distracted by the glare. The silhouette of a man was barely visible, just darker than the trees behind him. I dropped the cat and opened the door to the balcony.

"Who is that?" I said in a normal conversational tone. If it was a vampire, he'd hear me if I whispered. If it wasn't, well, he wouldn't hear me at all and wouldn't think I was crazy.

No one answered. I stared at the spot where I'd seen him, trying hard not to blink. He didn't move, standing so still I thought maybe I was just making it up. I thought I heard a noise behind me in the apartment. I glanced back for a moment and when I looked around again he was gone. I grabbed my keys and ran down the stairs, too excited to wait for the elevator. Out in the parking lot I could smell him. The scent was still strong enough to confirm that there had been a vampire around. I couldn't tell if it had been Shakespeare or not. The alternatives were scary.

Well, that whipped me right up. I went back upstairs and grabbed the vial of vampire essence, hanging it around my neck. A minute later Jai came out of the apartment and locked the door.

I was wearing a short black miniskirt with a green velvet bustier top, stacks of black metal bangles on both wrists, and, in a nod to how eager I was to move, a pair of low-heeled black boots that came up over my knees instead of my usual fearsome heels. My hair was pulled back in a thick braid and long black metal earrings hung almost to my shoulders. Looking punk and tough, I secretly clutched a post-it with driving directions to downtown.

I was going hunting after all.

The stone floor was warm when Vivienne stepped on it, though the heat faded away before it reached her icy heart. She drifted down the short hallway to the kitchenette Sir John had had installed with the rest of the basement rooms, her long white dress floating behind on a soft current of air. He didn't need a kitchen, so it was stocked only with her favorite things.

She selected an apple from the fruit crisper and marveled that such a fresh, perfect specimen could be found in June. When she was young, apples meant fall. Of course, this one didn't smell like much, and she missed the crisp sweet scent that always reminded her of burning leaves and cool nights. She bit it, laughing bitterly at the smooth ring her strong flat teeth cut into the flesh of the fruit. No long sharp canines for her. No, she was food. Food the Master would no longer eat.

Tears ran down her cheeks as she swallowed the bite.

"Vivienne," he said softly.

She swallowed again and brushed at her cheeks. He was suddenly standing close behind her, one arm wrapped around her waist, pulling her against his cold hard body.

"John," she could barely whisper.

"It is good to see you, Little Bird." He picked up her swirling hair and moved it to one side, baring her neck.

"Yes."

"I would taste you, if you'll allow me to."

"Oh yes." The apple fell to the floor.

Vampires can turn up anywhere, but the best hunting was downtown. The little vial of vampire essence rested between my breasts, keeping me secure. I backed Kristen's old Honda out of its parking spot and headed for the freeway. I'm not sure why I knew how to drive, or whether it was something I knew because Kristen knew how to do it. I always brought driving directions because I was afraid I wouldn't know how to get where I was going.

Getting to downtown was easier than finding parking once I was at Pioneer Square. I finally found a spot under the Viaduct, an elevated length of Highway 99 that had a gorgeous view of the water. Good thing, too, because when the big one hit, all those people who were on the Viaduct when it collapsed would have something pretty to look at on their way down.

Pioneer Square was the oldest neighborhood in Seattle. Once the center of the city, now it was home to artists, a few struggling retail shops, and the homeless, with all the soup kitchens and free clinics that are the necessary resources for that population. At night it was the place the young and reckless came to get their groove on, just like generations had done before them. The buildings were old and brick and mostly in good repair, though as you walked up the street every few feet was marked with the smell of urine. I hadn't walked very far before the smell of vampire blotted out the rest of the neighborhood stink.

Up ahead of me, three young vamps were walking arm in arm, heading for The Underground, a club on the corner of Second and Washington. Over the years it had been a dive bar, a speakeasy, a gay dance house, and a jazz spot. Its current incarnation was a discothèque where electronic music poured continuously from the speakers and packs of dancers shimmered under the strobe lights. Following the vampires, two boys and a girl, into the club, I watched as the girl peeled off to head to the ladies room. She was a tiny little blond thing in skater shorts, a midriff-baring shirt and high-top Converse shoes. Vampires don't pee, so I figured she was looking for dinner. Or breakfast. I went into the ladies room right behind her.

It was empty except for the two of us. Our eyes met. She reached for me. "Ooh, you're the one I was looking for," she said. I let her pull me in. We moved into one of the stalls.

Her head reached boob level on me so she hopped up onto the toilet to get a better angle at my bare neck.

"Don't hurt," I whispered, my mouth halfway between a snarl and a grin.

Her hands fumbled over me, as if she was trying to touch all of me at once. One hand slipped into my bustier and her fingers found my nipple. I sighed against her lips as she groped me then I reached down for Mr. Sticky. Her tongue was in my mouth when the blade found her chest. A moment later I was alone in the stall, her heart in my hand.

I pulled my top back up, settled the vial in its nook between my boobs, brushed the vampire dust off the toilet seat. Took a quick peek out of the stall. The bathroom was still empty. Lucky days. I tossed her heart into the wastepaper can and fluffed a few sheets of damp paper towel on top. Didn't want to scare anyone. Vampire hearts shrivel up after they've been cut out. I figured this one would be the size of a raisin in half an hour.

I painted on another layer of deep red lipstick and went back out in the club to look for her two boyfriends. They hadn't split up yet and were scanning the dance floor holding bottles of beer I knew they'd never drink. I walked up between them, wrapping my arms around their waists.

"Let's get out of here," I said.

We turned as a unit and I led them out of the club. Out on the street I looked for somewhere private. An alley ran behind the building The Underground was in, and I headed into it, leading them by the hands. It's tricky to kill two vampires when they're together. You have to distract one while you cut the other then get the blade into the second one before he figures out what's going on.

Out of the sight of the street, they made a Jai sandwich. One claimed my front half, applying himself to my mouth as if the color of my lipstick offended him and he needed to lick it all off. The other humped my butt and nibbled on my shoulder, his fangs scratching the bare skin. Simultaneously they moved in the direction of my neck. Oops, this sandwich didn't want to be lunch. I slipped down to my knees. The one in front of me was tall and black and looked to be in his early thirties. I opened the fly of his navy dress slacks and pulled out the tails of his cream silk button-down shirt. His pecker was next. I grabbed the base with one hand and went to work, sliding and sucking in long sure strokes. His friend stood behind me, hands on my shoulders, thrusting his hips at the back of my head. They might have been kissing over top of my head.

When vampire number one was almost ready, I stood up, keeping a hand on him. I kissed the other one, letting him lick his friend off my mouth. "Your turn next," I told him. "Get it out."

He reached for his fly and I reached for Mr. Sticky. Just as number one was about to find paradise, I had the blade in his chest and his heart in my hand. Number two looked up at me, his survival instincts completely clouded by lust, and then he was gone too. He died with his pecker in his hands.

I picked up both hearts and chucked them into the dumpster outside the back door of the club. It was apparently empty as they hit the bottom with a couple of squishy thumps. I turned towards the street, wiping my mouth with the back of my hand. Normally killing three vampires would make me all kinds of high, but not tonight. I felt sick, my mouth tasted like vampire dick, and I wondered whether any of them really deserved what they got. I mean, I knew the lady vamp wasn't heading into the bathroom for a Girl Scout meeting, but still. Maybe she only needed a sip. That thought curdled my stomach completely and suddenly I was retching.

This was not a glamorous moment. I was alone in an alley in the darkest part of the city puking my guts up. All the cute clothes in the world couldn't make this okay. I rested a hand against the damp brick of the building, feeling clammy and sore, and pulled the chain with the vampire essence off, dropping it into my purse.

Started the change back to Kristen. Stopped.

I wasn't alone. Vampire. Raw. Maybe a wild one. I looked up, nerves tingling because of the quick change to Kristen and back again. Saw him standing at one end of the alley, head turned to the side. Shakespeare's profile, with the firm brow and the long straight nose. Streetlights glistened on his curls. Very close, but not Shakespeare.

"I could tear your head off and let your blood mix with the bile and garbage and mud." His voice was Shakespeare's, too, but not quite. He moved enough to show the silhouette of the sword he was carrying.

I stood straighter, opened my arms a little. "Bring it."

"Bitch." He came at me too fast to see and smacked me across the face. My head hit the dumpster with a ringing crash. I landed on one knee, grateful I was in boots. Upright, Mr. Sticky and I had a chance. If he got me on the ground, I was done. His shadow towered over me.

"The moon's light begs mercy. She tells me to save you now that we might savor you together."

"So much like him, but not Shakespeare."

"Not Chaucer or Oscar Wilde, either, though they were both good men. I am Sir Hugh Robartes. You are nothing. You are dirt. You are dead."

"You're John's brother."

"Don't say that name."

His fist found my face again, knocking me back into the brick. I felt Mr. Sticky fly off into the shadows, then I was out.

CHAPTER 7

Herbert felt it, the loss, the separation. Jai had lost the blade. He knew it with the same assurance that he knew the sky was overhead. The vampire must have done something. He cast a web between bookshelves, staring into the glossy filaments that were barely visible in the minimal lighting that the mall required at night. This web could tell him many things if he had the time to read it. He didn't.

He looked for Jai, saw the strands of her life weaving across the surface, crossing every other story that the web held. He saw the vampire too, no, two vampires that had been linked since their birth. Bad news, both of them. He needed to get to Jai.

He stood very still, his multifaceted eyes dimming. In a breath, a man rose up from where the spider had been, a short man with cold black eyes and prominent teeth. He was dressed in jeans and a long black duster. Dark hair shot with silver fell long around his shoulders. He walked to the door of the shop and held his right hand just above the locked handle. When he heard it click he pushed the door open and went out into the mall.

I was out a couple of hours at least. When I could pry my swollen eyes open I saw I was in a hotel room, almost spilling out of my bustier top. I hadn't changed back to Kristen, which meant the vampire was somewhere nearby. A thin band of light showed where the drapes didn't quite meet in the middle. The sun wasn't up yet, but it wasn't full night either.

I was laying on my side on the bed, hands tied behind my back, ankles strapped together. My whole face felt bruised and there were tender areas along my ribs and shoulders. Before now, all the vampires I'd met had fallen down for me. Even the wild ones mostly just flailed around until Mr. Sticky got them. They weren't that hard to kill. Tonight, when the fists started flying, I'd folded, as if I had no idea how to fight. Unfortunate that I had to discover that little weakness the hard way. I preferred being the winner.

"Wake up, you." Hugh jabbed my shoulder. He came around the bed and into my line of sight. He shared his brother's build, profile, and hair color. The gloss of insanity in his eyes was all his own.

"I could kill you, you know. Right now." He reached out, cold fingers almost wrapping around my neck. "You think you can distract me with your flesh so poisonously sweet. He told me the secret was not to touch you. He told me..." He pivoted away and slammed his fist into the wall.

I always had something to say. Not now. I didn't want to set him off. Tried to look down to check for nipple peekage. My neck was too stiff to bend that far. He must have beat on me some more after he knocked me out. I didn't even want to think about what was hanging out from under my shortie-short skirt. Really wished I'd worn more than a thong. I concentrated on breathing slowly. If I could string two thoughts together, maybe I could come up with a plan.

"You're so close. You smell warm. Did you know that? Warm and sweet like moonflower on an August night."

My lips were cracked and stiff when I tried to talk. No sound came out.

"You lay there, and....and...I'm going to bring you to the Queen. It will please her." He stood with his back to me, both hands on the wall, his resonant voice strangled with an emotion I didn't want to identify. The wallpaper was a trendy 'sixties style floral. It was nice, except for the hole he'd just punched in it. The room itself wasn't large, and the bedspread under my face smelled clean. "We'll kill you together," he said. "He won't be able to stop us. He loves you—and I'll see you dead. The demon has kept you apart and now he won't find you in time."

I wasn't entirely sure who "he" was. Probably Shakespeare. I didn't say anything, didn't want to give him any ammunition. I could think of several ways for this to end. Almost all of them were variations on unpleasant.

"He was always first, you know?" His nails dug through the wallpaper, making tracks in the sheetrock. "He was born in a caul. It was good luck, our mother said. I was born with the cord around my neck. She said it would have been better if I'd hung myself."

He thrust clenched hands into his pockets. One fist started moving up and down. I *so* didn't want to know what he was rubbing. It was an instinctive reaction; when vampires were around me, they couldn't help but get aroused. I shut my eyes.

Can't touch you." He let out a soft gasp. "Not till I kill you."

He ducked through a door at the edge of my field of vision. I didn't know whether he'd gone into an adjoining room or the bathroom or the hall. I was just glad I didn't have to watch him jack off.

Robbie threw on some clothes, grabbed her car keys, and rushed out of the house. When the store didn't open, Security had called Kristen's apartment. When she didn't answer, they called Robbie.

She drove over to Kristen's as fast as she could. The tall evergreens that surrounded the complex looked dreary in the low overcast and light drizzle. The apartment was locked. Robbie had the key so she let herself in. Everything looked normal, except for the crazed cat doing figure eights around her ankles as she tried to walk around. She fed Petunia and drove to the bookstore.

The only thing unusual at the store was a large spider web that was blocking one of the aisles. Robbie reached out to brush it away so she could get back to the office, wondering whether Herbert was suffering from some kind of nesting instinct.

"Don't touch that," a sharp nasal voice said.

"Shit."

"You don't swear like that when Kristen's around." A short man with silver-streaked black hair came out of the office. Robbie shrieked. "Shut up. It's me. It's Herbert," he said.

"You are fucking kidding me." Robbie picked a book off the nearest display and threw it at nothing, just to feel better. "Why the hell not? You're a talking spider who's also a man."

"Listen to you, potty mouth. Kristen only thinks she has you trained. And don't throw shit around. You'll break something."

Robbie closed her eyes and pressed her palms into them for a minute. When she opened them, Herbert was still there. "Ok, so do you know why Kristen didn't open the store today, and why she's not at her apartment?"

"I have some ideas. I checked out a couple of things already and I'm about to head out again."

"I'm coming with you."

"No you're not. Stay here and keep the store open."

"Oh hell no. I'm coming with you."

Herbert glared at her then walked to the door. Robbie followed. Just before he turned his back to her, she caught the flash of a small grin on his face.

Once Hugh was gone and the scent of vampire faded, I turned back into Kristen. My arms were shorter and wider, and the change had shifted the bonds some. I thought if I worked at it I could get my hands free. I started sliding my arms back and forth, slowly feeling an increasing amount of play in the cords. Not all vampires go down the minute the sun rises, though only the oldest ones could stay up through the day. It had to be close to dawn. Crazy Hugh in the next room was going to have to shut it down soon, which would give me some time to try to get free. That thought was reassuring enough that I was briefly able to drift off to sleep.

"This is the woman I told you about." The sound of the vampire's voice and my sudden shift back to Jai was a harsh wake-up. "All you need to do is sit here and make sure she doesn't do anything."

"So you gonna pay me to sit here? Shee-it, look at them titties. I'm not sure I'll be able to keep my hands off those."

I guess vampires weren't the only ones impressed by my attributes.

"You do not touch her." Hugh shoved his companion into the door, his forearm under the man's throat.

"It's cool, dude. It's cool. Look but don't touch. I get it." The young man raised both hands in a sign of surrender.

Hugh backed away. "I will return near sunset. Do not leave her alone."

My window of opportunity for escape had gotten smaller. The young man, and by young I mean maybe eighteen, looked like Hugh had pulled him in off the street. His hair was in cornrows and his baggy jeans slid down over his hips, revealing green plaid cotton boxers. He sat in one of the two knock-off butterfly chairs that were down at the end of the bed. He stared at me for a minute, then whipped out his cell phone, and started texting someone. As soon as the smell of vampire faded I turned back into Kristen.

"Mother fucker," the kid said when he looked up and saw me. "You didn't look like that." I could only imagine what he saw. Shifting from Jai to Kristen hadn't cured my injuries. My eyes felt swollen and there was a gash in my upper lip. At least my privates were under wraps, covered by a tee shirt and a pair of jeans. I cleared my throat to see if I could speak.

"What the fuck is going on? You ain't the same lady." He jumped up and bounded over to the door.

"Well, yes and no," I started, my voice cracked and gravelly. "I am the same person. I just have a couple different looks." The truth was strange enough that he'd never believe it.

"I knew that dude was kinda weird. I fuckin' knew it. I don't need no hundred dollars bad enough for this."

"Listen, I know you're freaked out right now."

"No shit, I'm freaked out. You all can go play magician with somebody else."

"We're not playing. If you could, like, help me loosen whatever he's got tied around my wrists I'd really appreciate it."

"Oh, fuck no. I ain't touching you. No, no, no. I am gone. I am the invisible man."

"Wait, I really need help." I tried to make myself look particularly vulnerable. "If you won't undo the ties, could you at least call my friend and let her know where I am?"

"You'll have to ask that first lady who was tied up in here to help you. You people are crazy." He had a hand on the door, still tempted by the one hundred dollars. Then he was gone.

Good. I didn't need to add being molested by a teenage street kid to my list of traumas.

"And don't talk so ugly, either," I said as the door slammed shut. Kids these days and their four-letter words.

The strip of light between the curtains was much brighter, so I figured it was full daylight. I slowly moved my arms up and down, back and forth, feeling the bindings loosen. Every few minutes I got discouraged and thought about just lying there till Hugh took me to the Queen. Maybe she'd remember the deal she and Shakespeare were negotiating. Maybe she'd keep me safe. Maybe I didn't want to trust a screamingly powerful vampire who dressed like a flapper. And I really had to pee. I kept working at it.

It took all morning to untangle my arms. I sat up slowly, feeling the grooves in my wrists where they'd been bound. Tears came to my eyes when the blood starting running back into my hands. He'd tied my arms with leather-wrapped wire.

I'd have to remember that. Sitting up made me dizzy, so I took a couple of deep breaths and blinked until I could focus. When I had enough flexibility to make use of my opposable thumbs, I reached down to try to loosen the knots holding the thongs around my ankles.

It didn't take as long to free my legs and when I got down to it I learned that my left ankle was sprained. Jai's boots had probably helped keep the swelling down. Once the bindings were gone, a fat purple balloon obscured most of my ankle bones. Couldn't wait to try to walk on it. When my legs were free, I swung them over the edge of the bed. The need to find the toilet was powerfully motivating. It helped me ignore how bad everything hurt.

I limped into the bathroom only to find Hugh curled up on his side in the tub, dead for the day. Must have only been able to afford a single room. I closed the heavy white shower curtain and did my business, ignoring the fact that there was a guy in the room. A crazy dead guy. I washed my hands and splashed some cold water on my face to get the blood off. I dried it carefully with one of the hand towels, avoiding the swollen parts and the cut on my lip. The smell from the vampire had been enough to force the change, and a beat up mug shot version of Jai stared out from the mirror.

I went back over to the tub and looked down at Hugh. Without the crazy, he looked even more like his brother. That would make him hard to kill, even if Mr. Sticky was here and not out in an alley somewhere. I could hack out his heart. Maybe. Sir John's brother would be just as old as he was, and likely just as powerful. It could end badly.

I wasn't really the surgery type. In the end, I limped back into the bedroom, found the black leather backpack Kristen used as a purse, and left.

I wasn't used to being stared at as Kristen, so I did my best to look natural as I made my way up First Avenue, back into Pioneer Square. No problem, people, I always limp along covered in bruises, with my jeans torn and my hair alternating matted clumps with random frizzy bits. It was fortunate that the neighborhood was so colorful. For the most part, people left me alone, although one woman did offer me a sip from the mystery bottle she had wrapped in a brown paper bag. She looked like she was in worse shape than I was. I thanked her politely and kept going. My car was still under the Viaduct, complete with a parking ticket, and when I locked myself in the driver's seat I pinched my lips together so I wouldn't burst into tears.

"Let me refill your ice pack," Robbie said, hovering next to me.

"I want to give my ankle a break. Maybe stash it in the freezer and I'll put it back on in a while." I handed her the icepack, mainly to give her something to do.

She had already started supper, though I wasn't that hungry because I'd stopped at Dick's on my way home. It had been a long day.

"It's almost time for more Tylenol ," she said. I'd put her in charge of the medicine cabinet, too.

"It would be great if you could get me some," I said.

She bustled around the apartment. I stretched back on the couch, pillows from my bed tucked under my shoulders and my bad ankle elevated on a folded blanket. Petunia shifted slightly from her position draped across my thighs, her purr massaging my sore muscles. The sliding door was partway open and the smell of damp pine trees made me sigh. I was home.

"So I guess the store stayed closed all day."

"I'm sorry. Herbert and I spent the day looking for you. We found Mr. Sticky in an alley in Pioneer Square, but couldn't track you from there."

"You took Herbert to Pioneer Square?" I had a visual of her wandering up the cobblestone streets with a giant spider on a leash.

"Yeah. He's coming over later with Mr. Sticky."

"I'm missing something."

She stood under the arch that led into the kitchen, grinning because she had one on me. "Oh, yeah, he changed into a man. I thought you knew he could do that."

"Um, no. I've only ever seen a big black spider."

"He's kind of spider-ish as a man, too. You'll see. He'll be here soon."

"Great. Looking forward to it."

"I'm not the type to say "I Told You So," Herbert said—giving the phrase capital letters—as soon as he was through the door.

I wouldn't have guessed.

"I didn't think you were the type to stand on two legs, either. Shows you how much I know." My voice sounded a lot more tired than when I'd been chatting with Robbie.

"I warned you about that vampire."

"It wasn't Shakespeare. It was his brother Hugh."

"They're both bad news. I need to get Jai away from them." Herbert stood at the foot of the couch, the glare from the window turning him into a shadow except where his eyes glittered. Robbie stood behind the couch, watching us like she was at a tennis match. "Let me see her."

"No." Something about his intensity made me nervous.

"I want to give her Mr. Sticky back."

"Robbie, please go check on dinner," I said, conceding defeat.

Herbert smiled. Robbie huffed and walked into the kitchen. Herbert made a small sign with his right hand and a moment later, Jai lay on the couch.

The blanket that had supported Kristen's ankle hit behind my calf. I held out my hand for the blade.

"Kristen needs to give you up," Herbert said as he passed it to me.

"Go spin a web." I shut my eyes.

He moved, coming close enough to whisper in my ear.

"She can make it easy on herself. Or hard." He waved his hand in front of my face and brought Kristen back.

CHAPTER 8

Robbie came out of the kitchen with a bowl of chips for me.

"Are you guys through with the secret society shih—stuff?"

"Yeah baby," Herbert smiled at her. "All done. And you promised to braid my hair."

They went over to my tiny Ikea dining table. Herbert took a chair and Robbie stood behind him. Apparently she wanted to see if the silver streaks in his hair would make a pattern in the braid. I ate my chips one at a time and tried not to think about what was going on beside me.

Herbert was about four inches shorter than Robbie and with her being married and all, he didn't strike me as her type. When they were done playing beauty salon I booted them both out and hobbled to bed. It took a while to get to sleep because, in addition to the cuts and bruises, I kept feeling the three young vampires I'd kissed and fondled—and killed.

Saturday, the store was busy. Robbie had put in extra time at work since I hurt my ankle so that I could stay in the back and off my feet, though I'd drawn the line at having her chauffeur me to and from work. My only concession to taking the bus was leaving my car in the Safeway lot so that I didn't have the walk to my apartment. The ankle was getting better, though, and my visible bruises were fading. The invisible ones were still quite tender. I'd avoided Jai, and for her part she seemed content to hang out wherever it was she went when she wasn't me. I hadn't seen Herbert either, though Robbie mentioned him a couple of times.

The plan was that Corey would pick me up from work so we could do the dinner and a movie thing. It was an actual date, and since I'd had time to plan for it I'd had time to work myself up into a serious fit of nerves. I'd hit the Liz Claiborne rack in Macy's "short and round" section and had a new pair of jeans with a loosely tailored black blouse to show for it. I added a pair of chunky gold earrings and figured this was as cute as I was ever going to look. The clock moved ever closer to six p.m. which made my jaw clench tighter and tighter.

"So you haven't called Corey and cancelled yet? Herbert might actually lose the bet." Robbie stuck her head through the office door and smirked at me.

"You guys bet on me?"

"Hey, girlfriend, I got your back. I knew you wouldn't cancel."

"Go back to work."

"Easy there. You're going to make your hair curl even tighter if you don't take some deep breaths."

"Go back to work, I said. "I hear customers." I could still hear her laughing even after the door swung shut.

At five minutes to six there was a knock at the office door. My heart was beating so hard I might have keeled over just from that, even if I hadn't gotten snagged by the wheeled foot of the chair and landed hard on my bad ankle. At the sound of me thrashing around, Corey pushed open the door, catching me down on one knee and gasping.

"I fell." I looked up at him, caught on the point between laughter and tears.

"Here," he said, extending his hand to help me up.

We stood there for a moment. I kept hold of his hand and tested my left foot to see if it would bear weight. Not even a little.

"So, I had this thing happen earlier in the week that involved falling and spraining."

"I can see that." He brushed a few loose curls away from the fading bruise on my cheekbone.

"I was getting better and could almost walk without a limp until I just kinda fell on it again."

I was still holding his hand. He didn't seem to mind. In fact, he looked quite handsome in a forest green long-sleeved tee shirt and jeans. I might have been happy to stand there for quite some time, except I could feel the ankle swelling again and knew it would start to hurt soon. "I don't have crutches. I'm not sure how this is going to work."

"No worries. We have reservations at Marios. They'll have ice for your ankle, and after dinner we'll see how you're moving. I'm pretty sure there's an ace wrap in my first aid kit in the car. If wine, ice and a wrap don't fix it, we'll make it an early evening."

"You must have been a Boy Scout." I said as he handed me the purse off my desk and put an arm around my waist to help me out to the car.

The plan totally worked for me.

Vivienne stood next to the big brass bed. She wore only a shear camisole top and silky tap pants, her hair doubled up in a loose bun on the top of her head. Beside her the vampire stretched out, dead for a few more hours. She bent over him, her light top dropping down to reveal the shell-pink skin of her chest and the edge of her rosy nipples.

He didn't feel the kiss she placed gently on his forehead, or see the envelope she held. If he had seen it, he would have recognized who it was addressed to, and he would have noted the lavender wax seal on the back, a seal bearing the impression of a rose. A velvet robe was draped over the foot of the bed. She shrugged into it and tightened the belt before leaving him alone in the room. She let herself out the back door of the house and went around to the mailbox. Then she carefully placed the letter in the box and snapped it shut.

Dinner was great. I kept ice on my ankle and by the time we were done, I could almost put weight on it. Between my handicap and the fact that we hadn't agreed on a movie, we decided to go back to my place. Corey said he'd like to play nurse for a while. As long as he didn't want to play doctor, I was okay with it. We were spending enough time staring at each other, mirroring the other's silly grin, that I knew we might eventually get to the doctor stage. I just wasn't sure I was ready to put my naked body on display yet. I wasn't Jai.

I sat on the couch and he moved a stack of books in front of me, topping it with a throw pillow so I had something to put my foot on. Then he got us each a beer and sat next to me.

"No TV."

"Nope. There's a laptop in a case over by the door. If you can pick up my neighbor's wifi connection we can listen to Pandora or something."

That involved some more shuffling around. Eventually I heard the Eagles song "Peaceful, Easy Feeling" through the tinny laptop speakers.

Corey dropped back onto the couch next to me. "I logged into my own Pandora account, since I didn't recognize any of your music."

"I named all my stations after authors, based on what music I imagined the author was listening to when he or she wrote my favorite books."

"You're kidding."

"I read a lot."

"No shit."

"Please don't swear. It really bugs me."

He had the grace to look embarrassed. "Sorry. I know you mentioned that before."

I wasn't really upset, just wanted to make the ground rules clear. "No problem. It's just that my Dad was a writer and my Mom was an English teacher, and they were both determined that their girls would use language they could be proud of."

"I get that. My Dad was a high-school PE teacher, and my Mom's only job was raising me. That pretty much set me up to be athletic and successful."

"Or a drug-addicted loser who couldn't cope with the pressure."

He grinned at me over the bottle of beer. "Or that."

I gave in to a sudden impulse and ran my hand over the top of his bald head. "It looks so smooth."

He blushed. "Yeah, I, uh…."

"I like it. I like the way you look."

"I like the way you look too." And, to emphasize the point he leaned in and kissed me. His kiss was open, honest, a lot like him. He wasn't shy about it.

After a minute I stopped him so I could take my glasses off. That gave him permission to move in closer. We went on for several minutes, exploring lips, a little tongue, touching safe spots. Then he excused himself, clearly chagrinned, to make a pit stop.

As soon as the bathroom door closed I heard a thump on the balcony. Shakespeare was standing outside and with a wave of his hand he slid open the door. Vampire smell poured through. Jai stood up barefoot and in faded jeans, wincing a little when I put weight on the left ankle.

"Not a good time, dude," I said in a low voice.

"You've met my brother," he said as he stepped into the apartment.

"Yeah, he's a whack job who beat the shiz out of me then tried to add rape and murder to his list."

"Kris, are you talking to me?" Corey called from the bathroom.

"Get out," I hissed at Shakespeare. I heard the toilet flush and the water turn on. "Or get into the spare bedroom."

"Not your bedroom? Perhaps you and your guest will be using it later."

"Not joking, Shakespeare." I pulled Mr. Sticky out of his sheath to reinforce my point.

"You won't kill me."

"Right now I want to. Now go." He came further into the apartment instead of leaving. "There." I pointed to the spare bedroom door. As soon as the door shut I turned back into Kristen and Corey came out of the bathroom.

"You were talking to yourself," he said.

"Not really. Here, let's sit back down." I flopped onto the couch.

"Yeah, well maybe I should go." He glanced over at the door that Shakespeare had gone through, then at the open sliding glass door.

"Oh, no, you don't need to go."

"I'm going hiking first thing, so I need to get an early night."

"Sure." Oh no, oh no, oh no.

"Don't get up. I'll let myself out."

"Okay, um, thanks for dinner and all."

"Yeah. It was fun." He said it like he had a mouth full of glass, took one more glance at the bedroom door, and left.

One good thing about my apartment was that it was quiet. If the upstairs neighbor decided to take up square dancing, I might notice. Every now and then, the muscle-headed dude peeled his Mustang out onto the road, crunching gravel and squealing brakes. Other than that, the only sounds I heard were the noises that Petunia and I created. I sat still on the couch, staring into the brown glass bottle that held most of the beer that Corey had brought me. Petunia had hidden when Corey walked in, and was even less likely to come out with a vampire in the house. Smart cat.

The bedroom door opened behind me. Vampires are silent when they move, unless they want to be heard. It's their funky smell that gives them away. I turned into Jai.

"Your friend..." Shakespeare started to speak.

"Left. He heard you come in and he left. It was the first date Kristen has had in over ten years, not that she's been keeping track." I was surprisingly bitter.

"My apologies. Coming here was selfish."

"Ya think?"

"For four hundred years I've tried to help him find peace."

"Should have tried harder."

I shifted in my seat. The sheath that held Mr. Sticky in place wasn't meant to be worn while lounging. At least I was wearing jeans so I had a layer of protection under the buckles.

"It may take till I meet him in hell." There was a long silence after that. "Fifty years ago you would have killed him. I stopped you."

"That's looking kind of short-sighted right now."

"Instead, he almost killed us both. I have been tortured by regret."

"Bummer, dude. Meanwhile, I somehow lost track of who I am."

"Think, Jai. We were in Alabama, trying to stop a pod of vampires who were stirring up trouble during the early stages of the race conflict. We were trying to keep things focused on blacks and whites, not humans and vampires, trying to let the humans handle their own problems."

"Drawing a blank on that."

"When you had him cornered, I heard my mother's voice, begging me to take care of him. I asked you to free him. For me, you did."

"He doesn't seem all that appreciative."

"He drugged us, tied us down, and set fire to the house we were in. If the demon hadn't been nearby, to catch your essence as it left the hostess, you would have been lost."

"And you?"

"Went to ground. After four hundred years, I am difficult to kill, but it was a close thing."

I tried to remember. Seems like almost burning to death should stick with you. I should at least be nervous around candles or something. "I got a question for you, Shakespeare."

"Please call me John."

"Whatever. So, how come neither you or Herbert told me I didn't know how to fight?"

"Damn." He swore softly.

"Language."

"Jai, I wouldn't bet against you if you were taking on the Queen. You are a graceful and deadly weapon."

"Doubtful, because the other night I stood there thinking, 'wow, that hurt' every time your brother hit me."

"The demon has taken everything." His voice twisted in pain.

"Yeah, well, you may be right. I don't know. I can't flippin' remember. There's Kristen and maybe bits of the girl before her. Until I met you, I thought vampires were fun to tease and easy to kill. Even the wild ones couldn't hurt me."

He came closer to the couch, resting a hand on each of my shoulders. I glanced down at the gold ring. The green stones were glowing.

"Wild ones?"

"You know, the ones who are all dirty and crazy and can't talk or anything."

"Those sound like feral vampires, the ones the Queen referred to. I wonder who is responsible for their existence." His thumbs massaged the back of my neck.

I didn't want to talk about feral vampires or the Queen or any of that stuff because I was hopelessly stuck in the sucking hole that was me. "I don't care. They're not that much harder to kill than the regular kind."

"So sad, my love." I felt him lean forward, then his lips pressed the top of my head.

"Stop. Just, take two steps back." He did. I stood up, wincing on my bad ankle as I turned to face him. "I don't know anything. Herbert's a spider, when he's not a man, or a demon, or maybe some other thing I haven't seen yet. Vampires are evil, except you're not, and as much as it makes me crazy, I believe you when you say you love me. I think."

"Jai..."

I limped back a couple steps as he reached over the couch towards me. "No. Please. I don't want to mess around with you till I know who I am."

"I'll help you. We'll do it together."

"No. No way. I really don't know what the Francis is going on." I had to turn away because the pain on his face was too much. "You need to leave."

"Are you rescinding my invitation?"

I sighed from the bottom of my toes. "As silly as this sounds, yes, I'm rescinding your invitation."

He left without saying goodbye.

CHAPTER 9

I needed to debrief. I barely made it to work on time the next morning, then called Robbie and asked if she could have dinner with me after closing. It was Sunday, so the mall closed at six p.m. The busses didn't run as frequently, either, so between that and my tender ankle I gave myself a day of rest and drove to work. Since I had wheels and the weather was decent, Robbie and I decided to meet at Arnie's Fish House, a restaurant on the beach in the town of Edmunds. The thought of sitting on the deck in the sun with a cold Pinot Grigio made driving a bit and fighting the crowd worth the effort. And some calamari would be good, too. Work went quickly. It didn't seem to take much time at all before I was living my fantasy.

"We don't do this enough," Robbie said as the waitress delivered our drinks, a Lemoncello vodka with soda for her and a wineglass that might have doubled as a fish bowl for me.

"To having a life," I said as I raised my glass in a toast.

"To life," she echoed and we clinked glasses.

We each took a long swallow. The crisp mineral fruit taste of the wine was just as good as I'd imagined. I leaned back into the chair, taking my glasses off because the sun was creating a glare. I knew what Robbie looked like, and anyway, I'd only really need the glasses to read the menu. Clouds were moving up from the southwest. So far it was just the scout team, tubby white individuals with just a hint of grey to their underbellies showing bright against the pure blue sky. I listened the random slapping of water against the solid cedar posts that supported the deck and the clanking tackle of the sailboats that were moored nearby, relaxing in the salty breeze.

"The store was busy today," I said. Wasn't quite ready to tackle Corey.

"You know what I was thinking? You should start a blog that posts book reviews and upcoming store events and stuff. The store already has a Facebook page, right? It would be easy to link them."

"I barely have time to read, let alone write about what I'm reading."

"Just a thought."

"You could be my ghostwriter. I could tell you what I liked and you could type it up." I looked up to see her grinning at me.

"That's me, Kirsten's body double."

"Think I've already got one of those."

"Yeah, that. So are you going to tell me about last night? Did your alternate personality behave herself?"

I sighed, looking out over the water. "Sort of." I reprised the event of the night before.

"I can't believe he just left like that," she sputtered as my tale of woe wound down.

I was busy congratulating myself that I'd got through it all without tears. "Which one?"

"Either. Both. Men are such asshhhhivers. They give me shivers." She knew enough not to swear, and gave me a "get over it" look when I huffed at her.

"Shakespeare had to leave, I guess, when I took back my invitation. It's a vampire thing."

"Good thing we have Charlaine Harris to tell us how that works."

"I guess. I'm really bummed about Corey, though."

"I'll have to have Doug talk some sense into him. He has to know you're not the kind of girl who'd have a man sneak into your apartment and hide in the bedroom when you had another man there."

"Um, Robbie, that's pretty much what happened."

"Hello, extenuating circumstances. We'll put Doug to work on it." She waved at the waitress for another round. I wondered how my ankle would work after two glasses of wine. There was only one way to find out.

"So we need to get Jai's memory back," she said after the waitress left.

"I don't know how," I said, trying not to be all gloom and doom.

"Maybe I can wheedle something useful out of Herbert." She smiled primly. "I think he has a crush on me."

"Yeah, I've been meaning to talk to you about that," I said carefully, knowing I was going to go to a place that might piss her off. "I've noticed you two are getting kind of friendly." After all, what are friends for if you can't be honest with them.

"Seriously? You think that I and Herbert…that…he and I…he's a spider, for pity's sake."

"He's a spider who's turned into a not-unattractive man, if you can get over the fact that he's only about five-feet-four and has buck teeth."

"His hair is pretty sexy," she said, her voice dropping low.

Okay, that set my alarm bells off. "See, that's what I mean. You like him."

"Kris, I've been married ten years. I can draw the line at flirtation. Besides, Doug and I are busy working on a baby. We're going away next weekend for three whole nights of fun." She chugged some of her drink.

"I hope so, hon. I hope so."

It was nearly the end of the month and I had to put on my accounting hat. Robbie was in charge of taking inventory, which she did all day on Thursday. I worked the front of the store then saved all her work to a thumb drive so I could access it from home. I also took the stack of bills and papers that Robbie had been leaving on the desk under the black rock. Usually I stayed late at the store to do the books because everything's right there. Under the current circumstances, that seemed like a really bad idea. My fingers were crossed that nothing important was still in the office as I headed for the bus.

At home I sat on the edge of the couch with the laptop in my lap and piles of papers spread around me on the floor. Petunia was curled up next to my thigh. She reached out every so often to flex her paw so that her nails poked into my skin, which made me jump. The sliding door was open about eight inches, an old wooden yardstick blocking it so it couldn't open any further. I figured Shakespeare's evil brother wouldn't fit through the gap, and besides, I hadn't invited him in. There was no other vampire who scared me enough to worry about.

The air was warm and damp. Little in the way of breeze came through the door. I copied from one spreadsheet and pasted into another, trying to make everything come out even. Robbie had taught me how to pay the bills on-line, and when they were all paid, along with Robbie's salary and a slightly smaller amount for myself, I had seventy-seven dollars and forty-two cents to put into savings. So I did.

It was nearly closing time. Robbie had her laptop behind the cash register so she could track on-line orders while still keeping an eye on the store. She could pull things she needed from the floor stock and then send wireless commands to the printer to make address labels. The packaging was in the office, as were several racks of used books that she'd need to dig through after closing to complete the orders. Multitasking gave her a head start, at least. She was picking up address labels when Herbert came out of the back.

"Busy day today," he said.

"She emailed a ten per cent off coupon out to our regulars, so the on-line sales have been pretty good."

"You'll be staying late again to finish up ?" He came behind the counter, standing just a bit closer to her than was necessary.

"Are you ever going to turn back into a spider?" She aimed for brisk disinterest, missed the mark.

"I thought you liked me as a man." His weight shifted, moving him closer still.

She could tell he was checking out her ass and took half a step away from him. "The spider thing is a little disconcerting, but so is this...in a different way."

"You're getting under my skin, too."

She held up her left hand, showing off the ring. "Um, married."

"Um, demon." Herbert's smile offered a whole lot of promise. And something darker.

Life got better when I could walk without limping. I tried not to think about Corey, Jai mostly hid underground, and Robbie spent too much time with Herbert. We were passed the Fourth of July, which meant the sun didn't set until ten p.m. and the rain retired until October. I locked up the store in time to catch the nine-thirty bus, stopping out in front of Pottery Barn to stand in a shaft of rosy-orange light. I was safe from vampires, at least until the sun set, and we'd had plenty of customers. Things were good—as long as I didn't think too hard.

With a fairly empty head, I started moving towards the bus stop, pausing to let a motorcycle pass before I stepped off the curb. Jai screamed something in a language I didn't recognize. It scared me so bad that I jumped back, heart pounding. In that instant, the motorcycle ran so close to the curb I could see sparks fly off his footrest. He had revved it to near-highway speed, leaving me with an image of black leather jacket and gloves. About a hundred feet away from me he turned and looked back and I saw he wore a black helmet with a silver face shield. He gunned the engine a couple of times then took off.

"Thanks, Jai." I said out loud.

Don't know whether she heard me or not. We didn't have much internal dialogue so speaking directly seemed like as good an option as any. I felt her shrug, and then she was gone. I decided to call Robbie, since keeping her in the dark about things had more-or-less bit me in the butt. Doug was likely still at work so she'd have time to talk. I dug through my bag, looking for my cell phone, hoping the battery hadn't drained out of boredom since I used it so rarely.

I hit her voicemail. "So, Robbie, I just had a rabid motorcyclist try to run me down. I'm kind of freaked out. If you're around, call me. Please."

The sun was lower in the sky. I didn't know who might come after me next, and decided it would be in my own best interest to make that nine-thirty bus. I barely made it and spent the ride home trying to calm down. Deep breathing didn't work. Neither did reciting the Hail Mary or the preamble to the Constitution, which I could only do to the tune from Schoolhouse Rock. I kept the cell phone clutched in my hand, hoping Robbie would call back.

"The spider demon is a blight. He has nearly destroyed Jai."

"Let it go, John."

"You know I cannot, Little Bird." He stood up from the low leather sectional sofa that took up one corner of the library. Sconces sent warm light up the ochre walls. Vivienne was seated on an ottoman near him, her hair twisted into a chignon and her dusky purple halter dress a concession to the July heat. He ran a finger along one of her bare shoulders, making her shiver. The scent of roses drifted up from her skin.

"Then let me help you. Jai may have sent you away, but Kristen will see me."

"I would again be indebted to you, Little Bird," he said, playing with the damp curls at the back of her neck. For an ageless vampire, he felt weary and old. She stood and faced him.

"Feed," she said, gesturing towards her neck.

"Tell them they must find the focus, the object the demon uses to control Jai."

"Only if you do as I ask."

I had a visitor. Yeah, it's a bookstore, and people visit me all the time, but this one was more notable than most. It was Saturday morning and I had the front door open because of the heat. Sunlight coming through the front windows gave me a good look at all the dusty corners that hid out when the sky was overcast, and I was busy cleaning them up. Robbie and Doug had gone up to Whidbey Island for the weekend, ostensibly to look at property, but really, she hoped, to get pregnant. She talked a lot about having a baby, which I guess is what happens when you're in your mid-thirties and have been married ten years. I wouldn't know.

I was on my hands and knees, digging into a long-neglected corner, when a shadow marked the doorway.

"Kristen?"

The voice was familiar. I paused, my butt up in the air, feet halfway out of my sandals. I was wearing navy trousers that I hoped were dark enough to be slimming, if anything could slim my hips down from that angle. When my heart rate slowed down some I turned and sat back on my knees, adjusting the collar of my white eyelet blouse to make sure that private things stayed private.

"Corey?"

His smile was a little tentative. "You look like you're digging in the dirt like a puppy."

"Yeah, well, the cleaning service we have here doesn't always see things the way I do." He offered me his hand and I took it, letting go as soon as I was on my feet.

"I can believe that."

We stood staring at each other. Oh, no, this wasn't awkward at all.

"So, you doing some shopping?" I gave him a half smile. His bald head was shiny in the sunshine and I could see sturdy calf muscles between his hiking shorts and boots.

"Maybe." His smile warmed. "Look, I was thinking, if I'm an author and I'm listening to Green Day, what book would I write?"

"If you're a who and a what, now?"

"Like, if I was an author listening to Bauhaus or maybe Nirvana, I'd probably turn out to be Edgar Allen Poe."

"And if you were listening to Queen, you'd be F. Scott Fitzgerald."

"Exactly."

"So, Green Day. Maybe Hunter S. Thompson? Or Chuck Palahniuk? Let me see if I have *Fight Club*." I all but ran to the contemporary fiction section. "Hmm…not here. Watch the store for a minute and I'll see if it's in the back."

I burst into the back room. Things were organized because I was working, not Robbie. I opened our inventory list and searched for *Fight Club*. Corey stood in the doorway, one eye on the store, the other on me.

"Bummer. It's not here. I can order you a copy, though." I felt like an eager little puppy when I looked at him.

"That'd be cool. Then I'll have a reason to come back." We stood there doing that embarrassed staring thing again, until he finally took a deep breath. "Listen, about the other night, I'm sorry I freaked out on you."

"No, I think, I mean…"

"Be quiet, Kristen, and let me apologize." I shut up. "I realized that it was the first time I'd kissed a women who wasn't my wife, well, ex-wife, since the divorce. I let my nerves get the better of me, and I'm sorry."

"It's ok," I said softly.

A minute later we were holding hands through the doorway. Fortunately all my customers stayed out in the mall.

"I know that no one came in your sliding glass door and hid in a bedroom." He was looking at the floor when he said it.

I tugged on his hand a little to make him look at me. "Let's just say we survived our first date, so we don't have to worry about it anymore, and start over."

"Okay," he said.

With Robbie out of town for three days, it took me awhile to clear out the on-line orders. Ten o'clock came and went before I locked up for the night. The sun had set so I had to worry about vampires. Jai was restless, had been ever since Corey came in to the store. She got her way, too, because I was still in the mall itself when I smelled vampire. I ducked into the doorway of The Body Shop and turned into Jai, moving out into the mall quickly before the fruity soap smell turned me back into Kristen.

I was wearing a tight beaded tee with a sarong skirt that tied high on my hip. Which meant it was slit all the way up my thigh. Woo boy. I only had a thong underneath. It was one thing to flash The Girls, but my kooch should stay hidden, thanks. I hoped it would be an easy tag, because instead of feeling rough and tough, I felt sleazy. Not good.

From where I was standing I couldn't see the vampire. It wasn't Shakespeare, that much I knew.

"The Queen is watching," a voice said.

It seemed to be coming from behind the large corkscrew bush that dominated one end of the mall. I walked in that direction, wanting to get it over with. The shrub's twisted branches were still and threatening in the heavy air.

"Tell her I said 'Hi'." I whirled, sensing someone coming up behind me. No one was there. Mr. Sticky sprang into my hand. I kept heading towards the bush.

"You're not so frightening." The voice was deep, with the extra resonance that suggested a lot of years on earth.

"Come closer and tell me that."

Something flashed off to my right. I shifted my weight in that direction. Nothing. After a few more steps I stopped, waited, figured I'd see if the vampire could really leave me alone.

He couldn't.

It was a full frontal assault. He wasn't there, and then he was. "This is suicide," he murmured into my hair. His hands went up under my skirt and his cold fingers gripped my bare butt.

"You didn't have to do this. You could have left me alone."

Mr. Sticky was still in my hand. I moved the tip of the blade towards his chest, stopping against the thin fabric of his shirt. He was so busy rubbing his face in my hair and massaging my cheeks that he never noticed.

"C'mon dude, back off," I said, frustration twisting through my voice.

There was a moment when I could see him clearly. He was Asian, with gorgeous high cheekbones and straight black hair that fell across his forehead. I looked for the golden thread that Shakespeare had. Not exactly the same. Greys and browns and a little blue made variations in the darkness. I struggled, pushing into his chest with my free hand. Mr. Sticky wanted him. I didn't. Thinking about the feel of his heart made me gag and my gut spasm. Wonder if he'd notice if I threw up on his shirt.

I couldn't do it. My whole being refused to kill him. I threw Mr. Sticky away—bouncing it off the front window of the Express store—and sank to my knees with the vampire clutching at me. Folding over, I crouched down, hugging myself, pressing my forehead into the pebbled concrete walkway. He covered me, mumbling about wanting me, needing me, hating me. His voice didn't stop. The smell of his dead body overwhelmed me.

We'd been there forever and then some when I sensed another. Shakespeare lifted the Queen's messenger off me. The vampire clutched at me but Shakespeare was stronger. I heard one of them sobbing as they left.

I was alone. The air around me was warm, humid. I didn't move till well after I changed back into Kristen.

CHAPTER 10

You too good to kill vampires now?" Herbert was waiting for me when I got to work the next day. I was tired. I'd missed the ten-thirty bus, and at that time of night I'd had to wait an hour till the next one. Robbie was still out of town, so there was no one to cover the store.

"No, Herbert, I'm not too good, just smart enough to know we need to be more selective."

"There's no selective. Vampires are evil. You kill them." Herbert slammed his hand against the counter. I glared at him. "I can always take Jai and find a new hostess." He leaned into the counter, trying to look tall and threatening.

Too bad he was my height. "No. I like Jai. I'm not ready to give her up."

"Well I'm getting ready to take her. You remember that the next time you decide to play outside the rules." He disappeared in a puff of smoke. Black smoke.

I shrugged. For a demon he was sort of predictable.

☠

Robbie was awfully quiet when she finally did come back to work. Her trip was fine, she felt fine, it was all fine. Fine. She went back to the office and I started restocking out front. We hadn't been open ten minutes when Vivienne appeared in the doorway. She waved at me, gesturing that I should follow her. Guess she felt we knew each other well enough that she didn't need to drug me this time.

"Robbie, come watch the front for a minute." I waited till I heard Robbie move then followed Vivienne out the door. We walked a couple storefronts down the mall.

"Kristen, the Master sends a message."

"Hello, Vivienne. How are you today? The weather is lovely for this time of year."

She didn't get the sarcasm. "The message," she repeated.

"Alright, I'll bite. What is it?"

Robbie stuck her head out the door and watched us.

Vivienne's hair was pulled back and her eyes looked like fat plums in her bare face. "You must find out how the demon controls Jai. Find the focus, the point of control, so you can set her free."

"Herbert's a pretty secretive little turd," I said.

"Demon. Never forget that he's a demon."

I couldn't tell whether it was Jai or Herbert that was making her sound so tense.

"I won't. He has ways of reminding me."

"Good. You must set Jai free." She walked off.

"Tell Shakespeare I said thanks," I said softly when she was several steps away from me. She kept going without acknowledging my last comment.

☠

"I missed you this weekend." Herbert leaned against the register, watching Robbie as she unpacked a box of books.

Robbie had sent Kristen home early to make up for taking the weekend off. "I'm surprised you noticed I was gone."

She brought the empty box behind the counter and flattened it for the recycle bin. Customers floated around the store, browsing and chatting. Robbie answered a few questions and rang up a purchase. When the counter cleared she found Herbert standing close.

"Don't be naive, baby," he said, resting a hand on the small of her back.

He was almost touching her ass. She couldn't remember the last time Doug had touched any part of her. The whole story about going to Whidbey to make a baby was a crock. They'd rented separate hotel rooms so he could work all night.

Herbert's hand was hot, and she wondered if he was fueled by the flames of hell and whether all of him was that warm and what it would feel like to have his big front teeth playing with her nipples. That made several sensitive spots on her body burn.

"Come with me tonight," he said softly, apparently picking up on her train of thought.

"I can't stay out too late. Doug will come home, at some point."

"You can stay as long as you like." He never moved his hand, but she could feel his fingers brushing across her skin under her clothes.

She briefly worried that she and the demon were playing with fire, but that thought faded. Shaking the hair out of her face, she smiled down at him. She'd never had sex with someone who was shorter than she was.

After the motorcycle guy almost clipped me, I started keeping the vial of vampire essence handy, figuring that any ordinary human who tried to get me would be no match for Jai. I kept it in a pocket or in my work bag and slept with it on my nightstand. I also started carrying around a zip-loc bag full of garlic cloves. Ever since "the incident," or the night that Jai hadn't been able to kill the Queen's messenger, I decided it would be useful to have a way to keep Jai under wraps. I felt like Alice in Wonderland, with a baggie that could make me one thing and a bottle that could make me another.

Jai and I had been together more than ten months. At first I had been happy to let her take over, enjoying the excitement, the flirting, the fooling around. Killing vampires was just something we did. Being Jai was easy and I liked the hot clothes and the firm thighs. Then I met Shakespeare and started thinking about Jai as a person. I started looking for the good in vampires and suspecting there might be evil in Herbert. I started dating Corey. I hadn't read a book in two weeks.

I realized I was the main character in my own drama. That scared me.

Every bus smells the same, a blend of diesel and dirty humanity. I flashed my pass at the driver and sank into the closest seat. With my eyes shut, I felt the bus sway into motion, the headlights from the oncoming traffic flaring red through my eyelids then fading away. We made it about a third of the way home when the driver stopped to pick up passengers. They got on through the back door.

Shortly after they entered the dirty diesel bus smell was overcome by something different. Vampire. I grabbed my purse and fished out the garlic baggie. Since Shakespeare had given me a whole necklace of garlic, I wasn't sure what the minimum requirement to prevent transition would be. Maybe all I needed to do was hold one clove up close to my nose. Just in case, I held the whole baggie up to my face, hoping none of the other passengers were wondering what I was snorting.

There were many reasons I could think of not to turn into Jai, not the least of which was the three teenagers who were sitting across the aisle from me. Not sure how I'd explain the sudden onset of long legs and hair and boobs and oh yeah, the stabbing and the dust. It was hard enough to understand it all myself. The smell was getting stronger, so, trying to keep it casual, I shifted my weight and flicked a glance over my shoulder.

Three figures were behind me. One was an older woman. Her hair was long, with that Wicked Witch of the West thing that grey hair does if you're not careful. Then there was a kid who was tricked out like a wanna-be basketball star, Frankenstein-sized high-tops and all. Neither of them screamed vampire. That left the man who was in the last seat, his long legs stretched out into the center aisle. He wore a hoodie which hid his hair and put a shadow over his face. I had the feeling he was watching me.

It surprised me that no one else seemed to notice it smelled like one of my co-passengers was rotting to death on the bus. I chanced another glance backwards. Hoodie had moved up several seats. Everyone else seemed to be staring dead ahead, transfixed by the play of light and color as we drove up the highway. Maybe they wouldn't care if I suddenly jumped up dressed in something tight and black and stabbed someone.

"Hola puta." The voice was coming from the seat behind me.

I glance back and Hoodie had moved into attack position. Ok, well, I guess we'd see if anyone noticed the change. I tucked the bag of garlic back into my purse and turned around. When I met Hoodie's eyes, I was Jai.

The cotton-gingham sundress I was wearing was cut so low I thought The Girls were going to come out on their own and wave to their fans. I saw Hoodie's body stiffen.

"It's not polite to come up to a stranger on the bus and use profanity," I said, keeping my voice low.

"The Queen wants you."

"I'm sure we'll be best buds."

"Anyone who attracts the attention of the Vampire Queen is either very brave or very stupid."

We were driving without the interior lights on so it was hard to get a read on his features

"I'll leave that designation to posterity. Come join me up here." I patted the seat next to me.

He ground his teeth so hard I could hear it. My shoulder blades flinched with the sudden sensation of a blade pressing between them. I now apparently had my answer. My co-passengers neither noticed nor cared that I had turned into a completely different person and a vampire was now threatening me with a knife. Bunch of zombies.

"I could kill you right here," he hissed.

"Sure Hoodie, you're bad. Whatever. If I wanted your heart, it would be in my hand right now. I'm trying to cut down. Get it? 'Cut' down. It's a joke."

The knife pressed hard enough to break the skin until I calmly got up and moved to the very front bank of seats that faced the center aisle. There'd be no more sneaking up behind me. I turned back to Hoodie and stuck my tongue out at him. His face was still in the shadows so I couldn't tell if he sneered back. Loser.

The bus was pulling into my stop and I still wasn't sure how to get up to my apartment without bringing Hoodie with me. He'd followed me off the bus, and even from eight feet away the smell of him was enough to keep Kristen from coming back. The simplest thing would be to find a quiet corner and let Mr. Sticky do its thing.

If I could—I didn't trust myself. Crazy Hugh had proven I didn't know how to fight and the Queen's pretty Asian messenger had confirmed that I was losing my taste for killing. The fact that Hoodie had started carving a hole between my shoulder blades made it less likely I'd have an attack of conscience. I hoped. I wondered if he'd just stand there and let me stab him. If not, I might be in trouble.

Instead of heading for the shadows, I went to the light. The Safeway was open twenty-four hours a day, so I figured I'd hang out for a while and see if Hoodie had the balls to try to take me in the bakery aisle. I meandered through the store, occasionally sticking something in my basket. I was looking for stuff that might be useful as a weapon; canned goods, hunks of meat that were frozen solid, that kind of thing. Hoodie circled my position, never getting too close. He was the same height and build as Shakespeare and his brother, with a new and different smell. I hoped vampires had some magic that allowed them to alter their own scent. While thinking it was Crazy Hugh in a disguise was bad enough, worrying about yet *another* evil vampire trying to get me was infinitely worse. There should be a limit on that kind of thing.

I turned into the frozen food aisle, the cold making my bare legs prickle. I was trying to ignore the call of the Hagen Daaz when I nearly walked into another vampire. This one was tall, blond, slender, and dressed in skinny jeans with the cuff rolled up and a crisp peach polo jersey. He looked stunned when he saw me, although I don't think it was because he was all that impressed with The Girls.

"You smell Divine," he said.

I swear the D was capitalized. He took two steps towards me. I took two steps back.

"Dude. Grocery shopping?"

"For my servant. He likes Nutty Buddies."

I had a sudden vision of a burly man with close-cropped salt and pepper hair, a little goatee, and a manicure. I kept moving backwards because Blondie was getting closer.

"I don't usually like girls...like you." He dropped his shopping basket and lunged for me.

I dropped mine and ran. Hoodie followed us out of the store. I headed for the darkest part of the parking lot, Blondie right on my heels. When we were as far away from customers as possible, I stopped and let Blondie grab me. I angled myself so that he was behind me, crushing my boobs with his hands and gnawing on my neck. He was polite enough to keep his fangs in, which I appreciated. Small favors, you know.

Hoodie stopped about ten feet away.

I was betting that while Hoodie had kept himself from touching me on the bus, he wouldn't be able to resist if he saw another vampire with his hands in the cookie jar. It was a male territory thing. I was right. Hoodie stood rigid until Blondie pulled my skirt up and started rubbing my backside. Uh-oh. Sodomy wasn't something I had any experience with. It was a relief when Hoodie gave a roar and threw himself at us, knife blade flashing.

I ducked. Blondie grabbed Hoodie and threw him to the pavement, sending the knife sailing. As Blondie turned to chase me, Hoodie tripped him and they started into something worthy of WrestleMania, complete with body slams and head butts. I thrust Mr. Sticky in their direction a couple of times then decided that a sundress wasn't an appropriate outfit for killing. Not running away, really—kitten heeled sandals aren't made for running.

It was about a quarter mile from the Safeway to my apartment complex. Once I cleared the parking lot, Kristen took over, although there was no way she could have run the whole distance unless I was involved.

I grubbed through my purse till I found the vampire essence and hung it round my neck. Took three tries because I didn't want to stop moving. Jai came back in Nikes and some running shorts. I plan ahead. Sometimes.

The last hundred feet I was pretty sure I heard the machine-gun pounding of a running vamp behind me. Looking over my shoulder would slow me down. Figuring it didn't matter which one was back there, I ran faster.

A friendly neighbor was leaving as I got to my building. I flashed my key at him and ducked through the door, pulling it closed behind me. Elevator or stairs? The elevator started going up as I crossed the lobby, so I headed for the stairs. Because two flights of stairs were the perfect way to finish off a long run. Right.

Someone came thudding up the stairs as I fumbled with my key. I fought the lock and won, got into my apartment and threw the deadbolt before he came into the hall. Looked out the peephole. It wasn't Blondie. Darn. Hoodie stopped in front of my door, his face still hidden. It had to be Hugh under some kind of spell. Something slammed into the doorjamb. The lock held. I couldn't move. It was like staring into the eyes of a cobra. He swung an arm back and threw his knife at the door. It pierced the wood right next to the peephole, barely missing my nose. I sank to the floor as I heard his footsteps move away.

The story sounded even better the next day. I skimmed over some of the details, but still had Robbie shaking her ponytail back and forth in disbelief.

"So tell me this again. Two vampires fought over you in the Safeway parking lot and you managed to get away." She had a touch of eye makeup on, which was unusual for her. It made her already-blue eyes really sparkle.

"Yeah. I'm not sure if the one in the hoodie was Crazy Hugh or not. The smell wasn't right and I never got a good look at his face."

"What happened to the other one?"

"I don't know. I hope he's alright."

"Kristen, you're talking about a vampire who felt you up and was ready to come in your back door whether you were a willing participant or not. I'm not seeing your concern."

Maybe I had shared a little too much. "I was totally in control of the situation. Mr. Sticky would have gone to work before he'd done much more."

"Glad to hear it." Herbert came out of the office and leaned against one of the end-caps. "I was starting to think maybe you didn't want to use Mr. Sticky at all anymore." He looked sinister next to a display of Martha Stewart's newest book about good things.

"I told you I want to be more selective."

"And I told you to kill vampires. All vampires. Good ones, bad ones, ugly ones."

"I didn't know there were any ugly vampires," I said, afraid of the tone in his voice.

"You are trying my patience." He got close enough I could feel the heat radiating from him. "Jai kills vampires. That's why she exists. If you can't deal, then let her go." He reached for Robbie's hand, pulling her out the door behind him.

"Be back after lunch, boss," she called over her shoulder.

CHAPTER 11

So the thing about Corey was that he seemed just as happy communicating by email as he was with actually seeing me. He sent several messages a day, "Just checking in," or "Check out this link," or "Did you hear the Beatles broke up?."

Sometimes I felt like he thought I was part of some random stream-of-consciousness rather than an actual person, that I'd been incorporated into a life that was lived on the internet as much as on terra firma. On the one hand, it was nice to think about having a relationship that didn't require any real lifestyle changes. Of course, kissing him had been fun, too. I still wasn't quite sure how he'd managed to get past my rather substantial defenses. Now that he was in, I wanted him to take more advantage of his position.

But having an absentee relationship gave me plenty of time to stew over the fact that Crazy Hugh was still out there and to wonder whether he and Hoodie were the same guy, if you can call a vampire a guy. I was also worried about Robbie. She had less to say for herself and had more time unaccounted for. And the on-line orders were starting to seriously back up. Jai was putting pressure on me, too, although I had the sense that she just wanted to spend an evening hanging out and reading a book, maybe watching something on TV. It was weird.

It was a relief to finally get an email from Corey asking if I had plans for the evening. It was a Friday night and I'd extracted a promise from Robbie that she'd work so I could get off at a decent hour. I pinged him back an affirmative and in what felt like two minutes later he was waving at me through the bookstore door. Robbie was present and accounted for and the store wasn't too busy, so I grabbed my purse and left.

"There's an Indian restaurant in Bothell that's pretty good," he said as he opened the passenger door of his Xterra. He must have already moved the climbing gear because the seat was clear.

"The one that's just past the big fruit stand? I think I've been there before." Indian food has always been a favorite.

"Cool. It's not too far from the movie theater if there's something playing that we want to see. Or we could rent something and go back to my place." The fact that he kept his eyes on the road signaled the significance of his invitation.

"Sure. I'd like that," I said with a little smile. This was going to be fun.

It was. He wouldn't order the chicken biryani because he said it had bark and twigs in it. I couldn't convince him it was really only the cardamom seeds and pieces of cinnamon stick, so we compromised. We shared tandoori chicken and paneer so that he wouldn't have to eat twigs, and then I got to pick the garlic nan because it was my favorite. It didn't occur to me till too late that my breath might not be kissably-fresh after that. Oh well. We'd both be breathing garlic at each other.

The restaurant was dim and warm and smelled like curry. Corey drank a beer while I sipped some chai. I wanted some caffeine since I'd been on my feet all day. I was also afraid that wine and a heavy meal would put me to sleep before we got to the fun part.

"So Doug told me that you've been single a while." Corey followed that comment with a long swallow of beer. Tactful.

I looked into my chai, as if it would tell me what to say next. "It depends on how you define single, I guess." At least I returned his serve.

"Like, I've been single since my divorce three years ago. How long since you've been in a relationship?"

"None of your business." Defensiveness was so not the right call. If the waiter showed up with our dinners and saved me from this conversation, I'd double his tip.

Corey looked right at me, his eyes clear and honest. "I just want to know how fast to move."

"Meaning?"

"Meaning I want to take you home with me tonight and I want to get to know you a whole lot better. If I push, I'm afraid I'll come on too strong and chase you off."

He looked so cute and hopeful with his bald head and slouchy XBox tee-shirt that it made me blush. My head was a fractured mess of vampires and Jai and Corey, of bad scary things and sweet wonderful things. I honestly didn't know how to respond so I defaulted to the truth. Not something I had a lot of practice with when it came to men.

"I like you. You're the first guy since high school that could compete with the characters I read about in books." I grimaced. "Oh, that sounds pathetic."

"So I should take it slow."

"If by slow you mean that sex is off the table for tonight, probably. Well, possibly. If it means that we carry on communicating often via email but only seeing each other every few weeks, then I'd like to modify that."

He grinned. "Modify it, huh?"

"Like, we should hang out more. I think I'm ready to have a relationship in the first person. For a change."

"I can handle that."

"Besides, I thought you were supposed to be the fragile one since you just got divorced."

"I've had enough time to process things, I guess. I'm ready for someone new."

"I'd like to volunteer," I said and giggled into my chai.

"I thought you already had."

Robbie closed at nine-thirty p.m., after rushing the last customer through her purchase. Kristen would have found her three more books like the ones she picked out, hoping to sell just one more. Robbie wanted her gone. When the store was locked, she skipped back to the register and had the cash drawer out and in the office in a blink. Counted the money, pulled out a deposit slip, filled the cash bag, and locked it all in the safe.

Herbert was standing behind her as she finished. "You're coming with me." It wasn't a question.

She gazed at him, hungry and scared. "I shouldn't."

"You are." He pointed to the back wall. In front of the fully loaded bookcase, a circle of darkness started to form. The ends stretched, formed corners, and became a doorway into the black.

"Now," he pushed her gently between the shoulder blades.

She sighed and stepped into blankness. If it was a room, it was larger than anything she could imagine. The only tangible thing was Herbert. She was addicted to him, always seeking the approval of his black eyes, imagining the play of dark and light in his long hair.

"I want you naked," he said. She didn't move. "It's all fantasy, babe. You know I never really touch you. Clothes off."

She could feel him behind her, warm and solid, but he'd shown her that his human body was no more real than when he was a spider. The first time she'd come here with him, he'd shifted from man to spider to giant wolf to a creature of such horror she couldn't bear to think about it. She knew he'd simply take her clothes away if she didn't do it for him.

"Help me," she whispered, desperate to feel even the illusion of his hands on her body.

He chuckled softly. The last thing she saw before she shut her eyes was his twisted smile. Her clothes faded and she stood there, tall and lean and very naked.

"Raise your arms." Slowly she raised them and chains materialized, closing around her wrists. "God you have beautiful breasts." She shivered. "You know I'm not making you do anything that's not already in your heart."

"No." She felt him move closer, felt his hands and his mouth on her, fierce and hot. She knew that if she opened her eyes he'd be standing off to the side, and her brain would bend from the disconnect between what her body felt and what her eyes saw.

"What do you want tonight?" his voice whispered in her ear. She could feel his breath on her skin. "Do you feel like dancing?" In her mind she saw the glare of a spotlight on a single brass pole, heard the murmur of a crowd beyond the lights. "Or maybe you can be a concubine for my sheik."

They were standing in a tent made of colored silks. She hands were free and she reached down to touch a slim chain around her waist holding shear sashes that almost made a skirt. Beaded necklaces hung down cool and smooth between her breasts. She felt hands on her shoulders that forced her to her knees.

"You are such a lovely baby," he said, and she groaned as something solid forced its way between her legs, bending her forward.

She wondered if it counted as adultery when your lover never touched you.

In the end, Corey was a gentleman and brought me home. We mashed in the car like a couple of teenagers and though I invited him in, he declined, saying he was meeting some people for an early-morning bike ride. My feelings weren't too hurt, and by the time I'd locked the apartment door I was glad to be home alone.

Petunia met me with a series of wailing yelps, telling me plainly that she didn't think much of my social life interfering with her meal times. I fed her, changed into flannel jammies, brushed my teeth, and got into bed. Just as I was drifting off I remembered the vial of vampire essence. It was still in my purse. I hauled myself back out of bed and got it, setting it on the nightstand under my lamp as I crawled back under the covers. A couple minutes later Petunia joined me, sidling in between my chest and my upper arm, then reaching out to knead my armpit.

"Really, cat, it's soft enough up there." There was no stopping her, so I gritted my teeth until we both fell asleep.

If I was dreaming, Petunia chased the dream away when she gave a screeching howl and flew off the bed, slicing the side of my boob with her claws on the way by. I reached over to turn on the light just as the blade skimmed my cheek and embedded itself in my pillow. Instead of the light, I reached for the vampire essence. A moment later Jai pulled Mr. Sticky out of its sheath and sat up in bed.

Just beyond my feet I could see the silhouette of someone flat-chested—so probably a male. Or an unlucky girl. I stood up and raised the blade. The figure dodged, feinted, and threw another dagger in my direction. I leaped off the bed and chased it out into the living room. It went through the open sliding glass door and leapt off the balcony.

"Can I swear now?" I asked Petunia, although she was hiding and likely would be for a week. "Because if I could swear, I'd probably have something pretty effing colorful to say." I looked at the clock over the stove—three-fourteen a.m. I walked out to the balcony. No one around. Too late to call Corey. Too late to call Robbie. I thought about going back to the store to talk to Herbert, then decided it wasn't impossible that he was the one throwing daggers. I hadn't noticed vampire smell before I'd thrown the chain around my neck and turned into Jai. But it all happened so fast maybe I'd missed it.

I wasn't staying home alone though. I closed the sliding glass door and locked it, blocking it in place with the yardstick. I could see my reflection in the glass, all big eyes and short shorts, The Girls out loose in a tank top with the vampire essence hanging between them. Common sense time. I dug through the closet until I found an old pair of Kristen's jeans that were just a little short and a little wide for me. If I rolled up the hems to make them clam digger length and let the waist ride low on my hips, they looked okay. I pulled on an old sweatshirt that ended about an inch above the waistband of the pants and slipped into a pair of flip-flops. As I locked up, I wondered if Shakespeare still lived in the neighborhood.

I jogged along the road back towards the Safeway, jumping at every creak and grumble from the trees on either side of me. It took a good quarter mile before I stopped flinching at shadows, convinced they each concealed a knife-wielding nutcase. When I got out to the highway I knew it was late because even Dick's had closed for the night. Very few cars passed as I walked along. One guy slowed down and unrolled his window as he got near me, which made my heart cramp. He drove on when I shook my head. Sometimes hookers worked stretches of this road. It was awfully late for any other kind of pedestrian.

Down at the next light I turned right. I remembered that Shakespeare's house was on an undeveloped piece of property between the highway and the next big development. It should be a couple hundred yards up the road.

It was more like half a mile. I'd nearly given up hope when I saw it. No lights were on. Even the streetlight in front of it had burned out. It made sense because, if I was a vampire, I wouldn't want my house looking like a Thomas Kinkaid painting. I started poking around, wondering how to attract Shakespeare's attention.

Knocking on the front door seemed too obvious. Predictably, no one answered when I did. I crept around back. Nothing. I stood at the back door and breathed deeply, trying to catch a trace of vampire smell. It was there, faint and old. I was in the right place but on the wrong side of the door.

Thinking I might find a separate entrance, like the door to a bomb shelter, I made a circuit of the back yard. There was an old swing-set in the middle and a small shed in the back corner of the lot. I walked around the shed slowly, then nearly jumped out of my skin when Vivienne came wafting around the corner of the house from the front yard.

"The Master says to tell you you're welcome to come in." She sounded bitter.

"Thanks. I'd like that."

She pulled a key ring from a little pouch in the side of her fluid silk skirt and opened the back door.

"Vivienne, leave us," I heard Shakespeare's voice from below.

She sniffed and motioned me down the stairs with her head. The lock turned behind me as I went down.

"You didn't need to send her away," I said when I got to the lower level. I was in a small foyer with rooms opening off two walls and a hallway in front of me. It was lit by a row of amber sconces that lined the walls. Large slate tiles covered the floor.

"Come into the library," he said then started walking down the hall.

I followed. Since I'd come crawling to him, the least I could do was be polite. "Listen, something happened tonight that really scared me, and it isn't like I needed some big strong vampire to save me or anything, but I think there's going to be a fight, and I need someone on my side who can handle himself."

"Sit down, Jai." He sank onto one end of a sectional sofa. I chose the other end. "Tell me what happened."

I took a moment to breathe. My heart rate was slowing down for the first time since Petunia had screeched at me. I bowed my head for a moment then looked up at him. He was so amazingly handsome I forgot what I'd been about to say. Focus, girlfriend.

"After Kristen went to bed tonight someone broke into the apartment and tried to stab her."

"While she slept?" He sounded appalled.

I nodded. "I didn't get a good look at them because they were all in black and they were moving fast. I'm not even sure if they were male or female. There's been other stuff happening too." I figured if I was going to trust him to help me, he should know everything.

"Such as?"

So I told him about the motorcycle and Hoodie, and about how unhappy Herbert was with Jai because she hadn't killed the last couple vampires she'd faced. "This is bad, John. Kristen's pretty cool, in her own dorky way, and I'm worried that someone's trying to kill her."

"She won't give you up."

"I think she's getting closer, although I don't think she realizes how trapped I am. Oh, I can't believe I just said that." I covered my mouth with my hands.

"It's alright, Jai." Shakespeare appeared at my side, gently pulling my hands away from my face.

I laughed. "Sure it is. If Kristen gives me up, Herbert will just find another desperate woman who likes a cheap thrill. I'm pretty sure that's how he's been operating since your brother set the fire."

"We must not let him do that."

"I won't remember it anyway. He's wiping me clean with every shift." My voice sounded as hopeless as I felt.

The big sucking hole was back and I was desperate not to drown in it.

"When we were together, we found hostesses who were willing to give you most of their time. That helped you retain yourself."

"Okay, that's kind of creepy. How did you do it?"

"There were...compromises." He shrugged in a way that showed how long it had been since he was human. "We made it work."

I looked up at him. "So, you'll help me?"

"I am ever yours, my lady."

He tried pulled me close. As much as I wanted him to hold me, I backed away.

"Nothing physical yet. I'm sorry, I just can't. I've been pawed and groped and—" I choked on a sob. "Please, let's just hold hands or something."

"I'm going to kill the demon." He said it matter-of-factly, as if he'd just told me he was going to take out the trash. "I'm going to retrieve your focus and unbind the spell that's holding the demon together."

"Then who will I belong to?"

"Yourself, my love. Yourself."

The rest of the night I slept on Shakespeare's sofa. He sat near me while I drifted off, his fingers tangled in my hair, the only contact I could tolerate. When I woke up he was gone and Vivienne was sitting on an ottoman, looking at me like I was a pile of offal. Better than coffee for starting the day off right. She showed me out, even offering to drive me back to my apartment. I declined. I took the necklace off and Kristen walked home.

The jeans Jai had worn didn't quite fit, so I had to leave them unbuttoned. They were tight enough on my hips that they stayed up while I walked. At least I wasn't parading around in flannel jammies. The sun said it was nearly time to open the store. I got home as quick as I could, changed into work clothes even faster, and drove to work.

We opened fifteen minutes late. I'm not sure whether I missed any customers, although when I booted up the computer and checked the website, I saw there were as many complaints about orders not received as there were new orders. I called Robbie and left her a voicemail, trying to be oblique so she'd know I was pissed but wouldn't exactly know why. Cool. No sleep, no coffee, no sales. This day was getting better and better.

I cheered up significantly when I got the first email from Corey. He'd gone for his bike ride and wanted to know if I had plans for dinner. Before I could reply, he turned up in the shop, wheeling his bike through the door.

"Hope I'm not being a pest," he said, looking sheepish.

"Not at all, I just —" I yawned really big.

"You look tired. Rough night?"

"Long story." A cluster of women came in. One headed for the cookbooks, the other two went to the mysteries. Corey leaned against the counter looking nice in his tight biker shorts, waiting patiently while I suggested two authors whose work was similar to one customer's favorite. Sold two of the three women the books I suggested. Happy customers made a happy Kristen.

"You're good at that," Corey said when they left.

I shrugged. "I've been at it a while, and I like getting people to read."

"So last night—"

"Guess I had a bit of a break-in."

"The hell!"

"Dude, please."

"Sorry, it's just, somebody tried to break in to your apartment. That pisses me off."

"They actually, kinda, got in."

"What?" He slammed his hand on the nearest stack of books.

"Well, it was okay because they left when I woke up." I left out the part about the knives. Sue me.

"So, am I spending tonight at your house or are you coming to mine? Because you aren't sleeping by yourself."

"Um…" Part of me wanted to insist that I was fine on my own. The rest of me thought the first part was crazy and wanted nothing to do with being alone in bed. "As much as I hate playing the damsel in distress card, either would be fine." We decided that it would be less traumatic for me to stay with him.

Corey was still hanging around when Robbie showed up. She looked even worse than I did, her eyes hollow and grey. She wore a long-sleeved shirt, which was odd for July, and as she moved around I thought I noticed bruises on her wrists. I didn't want to ask what the heck was going on when Corey was around.

"I'll be in the office, catching up on the orders," she said, cutting through the store almost faster than was polite. "Then I can close tonight so you two can go do whatever it is you're scheming."

"If you want to, that would be great."

"No problem," she said, disappearing into the back.

"She looks pretty stressed," Corey said.

If a computer geek picks up on it, something must be really wrong. Robbie and I were going to have a chat soon.

It didn't happen that day. Corey took off on his bike, and then the store filled up. I spent the rest of the afternoon running from customer to customer. I almost pulled Robbie out to help on the floor, but we were so behind on the orders I was afraid to interrupt her. By six p.m. I was ready to drop in my boots. The crowd had cleared, so I went to check on Robbie.

"Suppertime," I said, poking my head through the office door.

She didn't look up from the computer. "Almost done."

"If you're too tired to work the floor, it's no biggie."

She glanced at me then went back to the screen. "It's cool. I don't mind closing."

"Okay then," I said, backing out of the door. I thought I heard voices murmuring as it swung shut. If it was Herbert, I didn't want to talk to him unless I had to.

Twenty minutes later she came out of the office carrying my purse. "Go find Prince Charming," she said with a grin that almost looked normal.

"Really? Thanks," I said, so tired I was almost asleep on my feet.

"Go."

I went. Corey had left me directions and said he'd have dinner ready when I got there. I drove home to feed Petunia and grab a change of clothes. And my toothbrush.

CHAPTER 12

Robbie focused on straightening the display beside the cash register, trying to ignore Herbert.

"Close early," he said, sitting cross-legged on the floor behind the counter. The customers couldn't see him from there, and he could distract her while she worked.

"Can't." It was hard not to look at him.

"You know what happens when you don't do what you're told."

"Stop it," she said, rubbing the fingers of one hand across the other wrist. Two women came up to the register. She rang up their purchases, wondering why she didn't tell Herbert to go away.

"I need you to do something for me," he said after the customers left.

"I already have to do all kinds of stuff for you."

"This is something special." He rose and came over to stand close, running his fingertips along her spine. It felt like he'd lit a match to a fuse than blazed down below her waist. "Promise me, or it'll hurt. Bad."

She shivered at the sound of his words. "Okay, I promise. What is it?"

He told her what he wanted her to do.

Corey and I enjoyed playing house. We fell into a little rhythm. I went by my apartment to take care of Petunia, both of us worked all day, then we took turns making dinner. After dinner we watched a movie or read to each other. Every night we went a few steps further down the path to adult relations. It was an issue of when, not if. He had such talented hands that I wasn't in all that great a rush. It would happen when it was right. In the meantime we were having fun. If it weren't for Robbie's haggard appearance, I would have blocked all about the bad stuff right out of my head.

On my fourth night as Corey's guest, I smelled vampire when I got to his house. I parked on the street, and right after I smelled him, I saw Crazy Hugh standing under a tree at the front corner of the yard. I had to get past him to get into the house so I grabbed the baggie of garlic that was still in my purse. I wanted to make it inside without turning into Jai. Corey's car wasn't home yet even though it was ten p.m. The house was dark except for the porch light.

"Foolish woman. I could kill you before you knew what had happened. At least Jai would slow me down."

I lowered the bag of garlic. Jai looked up.

I didn't stop moving to the front door. "What's up, Crazy?"

"I'm going to bathe in your blood and laugh while you die."

"Funny, I thought you were the dead one. You need to get over this...thing. What did I ever do to you?"

"You will learn to fear me," he said, coming right up close faster than I could see.

I had my hand on the doorknob. "Doubtful."

"Hugh," Shakespeare's voice came out of the darkness.

"John," I said, turning towards him.

"No," Hugh shouted, flying towards his brother.

I reached for Mr. Sticky and headed towards them. They were circling each other. Hugh reached for me when I got close enough. Shakespeare did the same, and on a dime his brother turned and trapped him in a headlock.

"No," I gasped.

"Drop the blade," Hugh said through gritted teeth. He held a dagger to Shakespeare's throat with one hand and a fistful of his hair with the other. "Drop it or I'll start cutting."

"He won't really harm me, Jai. Go inside," Shakespeare's voice sounded surprisingly normal. Hugh rammed his knee against Shakespeare's legs, forcing him to the ground. The move stretched Shakespeare's head back, exposing his neck.

"Yes brother, I can tell you're in control of the situation." Hugh laughed as he spoke.

"Go inside, Jai."

"Ah crap," I said, and threw Mr. Sticky, hard, like a javelin, aiming at Hugh.

Losing it would really piss Herbert off, but I didn't know what else to do. It slid all the way through his shoulder, stopped only by the hilt. He dropped down onto his butt, letting go of both his knife and Shakespeare. He was down on the road, knees bent, leaning on one elbow while he tried to pull Mr. Sticky out with his other hand. Shakespeare cuffed him in the head as I reached in and pulled out the blade. Good. Wouldn't have to worry about Herbert's temper.

Shakespeare dragged Hugh to his feet. A slow stream of maroon blood ran down the wounded vampire's shirt.

"I thank you, Jai," Shakespeare said. "Again you have risked yourself for me."

"Yeah, well, if I can turn up at your house and beg for help in the middle of the night, stabbing your crazy brother was the least I could do."

Before I could stop him, he leaned over to me and kissed me full on the mouth. Sweet. I couldn't move. He backed away and frog-marched his brother up the street. They were only a couple houses down when I turned back into Kristen.

It wasn't until I was behind the locked front door, shaking so hard it made my teeth chatter, that I thought about what might have happened if Corey had come home while they were here.

Lying in Corey's arms that night I made a decision. He snored softly, smelling warm and slightly sweaty, but in a good way. I knew Shakespeare was standing out in the yard, watching the house, keeping Jai safe. I wanted them to have what Corey and I were having. On some level I could tell that Jai understood what she was missing. This was a new realization, and it made me feel awkward, like Jai was somehow my prisoner. I needed to find the focus object to get Jai free of Herbert.

When I left Corey's the next morning, I drove to my apartment to feed Petunia. Robbie had opened the store. I wasn't planning on arriving till noon, so I had time to play with her for a while.

Things in the apartment were right where I left them, everything in its familiar place. Strangely, Petunia didn't attack me as soon as I came through the door. She'd been so lonesome that whenever I did stop by she turned into Velcro-kitty. Corey didn't have pets, though I thought he was a dog-man. We weren't ready for the kind of commitment that sharing a cat would require. I looked around the apartment, calling for Petunia. She didn't respond. Opening a can of cat food was an almost-guaranteed way of bringing her out of hiding. That didn't work either, so I checked her favorite sleeping places. It wasn't until I pulled back all the chairs from under the dining table that I found her curled up on one.

I poked at her. She didn't move. "Hey, cat, wake up. It's breakfast time." Still nothing. I reached for her then pulled my hand back when I noticed a puddle of kitty vomit near her mouth. Something was very wrong. I couldn't tell if she was breathing, which almost stopped my heart. I grabbed her, ignoring the slime, and pulled her into my lap.

"Petunia, what's wrong? Oh my God, what's wrong?" Choking sobs battled with gasping gulps of air as I held her. She drooped across me like a limp noodle, but at least she was still warm. A fat tear dropped off the end of my nose. "You can't die, Petunia. You just can't. If you do, it'll kill me."

Cradling her in one arm, I grabbed the phone, calling Corey first and then the vet. My hands were shaking so hard I could barely dial. I bundled Petunia in a towel and drove to the vet's clinic. Corey met me there. She was barely alive. The vet told me she'd been drugged. Only my morning visit had saved her. She was so out of it she'd have stopped breathing by lunch. The vet questioned me for over half an hour, trying to figure out where Petunia had got the poison. I couldn't tell him.

Once she was stable, I had to go to work. Robbie still had on-line orders to catch up on and someone needed to watch the store. I made the vet's assistant promise to call me if Petunia's status changed. Leaving her was as hard as anything I've done in life. Corey took my hand and walked me to the car. He held me for a long time before I could find the strength I needed to drive away.

"This has got to stop," I said to Robbie.

She was slumped over, her elbows on the countertop by the register, her hair stringy, her face in her palms.

"No shit," she sighed.

I was too strung out to correct her. "It's because of Jai. Everybody wants a piece of her."

"You should let her go, then."

"Not unless I know she's safe."

She stifled a yawn. "Shakespeare got rid of his brother."

"I don't think Hugh's behind all of it. I mean, he's more of a blunt instrument, you know? He's Thunderdome in the Safeway parking lot, not poisoning my cat and running me off the road on his motorcycle, or throwing a dead rat at my balcony, for that matter. That kind of stuff is about messing with my head, and he's not that subtle."

"So who do you think it is?"

It occurred to me that it might not be wise to answer that question in the store, since Herbert was one of my main suspects and would likely hear me. "Ah, I don't know. Let's just get to work." I said out loud. Then, on a post-it, I wrote, *Hebert might be. I need to figure out what the focus is, the object that he uses to control Jai.*

She looked at me for a long time then walked into the office. When she came back out, she locked the office door, tears spilling down her cheeks. She took the stack of post-its from me.

After sex, Herbert likes to boast, she wrote. *He says the focus is the black rock, our paperweight. He says that if you won't give Jai up willingly, he'll kill you. The rock is gone, Kris. Get yourself someplace safe.*

I stared at her, unsure whether to thank her for sharing or hate her for keeping this from me.

"I'm so sorry," she whispered, then started to sob. "I should have told you already."

I crumpled the note and put it in my pocket, then took the vial of vampire essence out of my purse. "Keep the store open as long as you can," I said, and slipped the necklace on.

When I appeared—where Kristen had just been—an inch taller than Robbie and wearing a black slip dress with black leather sandals that buckled up the top of my foot like gladiator shoes, Robbie looked stunned. I couldn't think of anything to say to her so I turned and left the store.

"Vivienne, we must talk."

"Of course, John. Whatever you say."

Outside the sun had just set. It was nearly ten p.m. She went into her day room, the best-lit of all the rooms in John's lair. He followed her in. She stood with her back to him.

"Likely Jai will need a new hostess soon."

"And the demon will move her and then we'll chase all over the country trying to find her." She shrugged. "We've done it before."

"This time will be different. It must be."

She turned to face him. "How?"

"I will have the focus, and the demon will not. I will choose her new hostess."

"And then I'll get to watch you make love to another woman. If you're asking whether I'm interested in that, the answer is the same as it was the last time you asked it."

"I'm asking you to be the hostess."

Rage contorted her face as she surged to her feet. "You can't be serious. You would ask me to obliterate myself, to let her personality take me over?"

"Little Bird, please. I can never give you what you want. All these years you've waited for me to love you, and while I depend on you for my very life, I cannot love you as a man does a woman. As Jai's hostess, you'll share your personality with hers. She won't smother you entirely."

"And when you thrust into her and moan with pleasure, I'll get to share in it. Poor little Vivienne always staring through the window."

"When I thrust into her, I'll be thrusting into you, in the only way I can. I'll know it, and you'll feel it. We vampires are not meant to love our food. Even after two hundred years I simply cannot do as you ask."

She glared at him, half hidden by the wave of hair she flipped down over her face. After a moment he realized she was not going to say anything, so he kept talking. "This is not perfect, I concede. Remember that we've tried other ways that are also imperfect. By my word, I beg you to consider this alternative."

She did not respond. After a few minutes, he left her alone.

CHAPTER 13

Vivienne waited until she was sure John was gone. Then she went to the small desk in the corner and brought out a sheet of heavy cream-colored paper. The last time Sir John had found Jai, Vivienne had stayed until she could no longer stand the sight of them mooning over each other. She wouldn't do it again. It was time to put her escape plan into action. With the first letter, she'd drawn the arrow. Now she'd let it fly.

Robbie would keep the store open for Kristen or she wouldn't. Herbert would kill her for telling Kristen about the stone, or he wouldn't. Robbie's loyalty was suspect, and Herbert was, well, a demon. I was done with both of them. The hold Herbert had on Robbie was a bad thing, and I wasn't taking the vial of vampire essence off till Kristen and I were both safe. I think we both knew that it was getting harder to see where one of us began and the other ended. Kristen was a nice girl and all, but I had Mr. Sticky and she didn't. For now, I was driving the bus.

I headed south on Highway 522, which eventually connected with Interstate 5. From there I thought about driving north towards Bellingham, although I was afraid I'd turn chicken and keep going till I hit Canada. I could drive south instead. Kristen would enjoy browsing Powell's Bookstore in Portland for an afternoon, and then in a day or so I could get to that other foreign country, California. No. I needed to be somewhere that the bad guys couldn't find me, but not that far away, so it was wiser for me to stay off the freeway.

North Seattle boasts the first indoor shopping center ever built in this country. Northgate Mall is right by I-5, and while the temptation presented by the freeway was hard to ignore, I decided that shopping was a reasonable distraction. Turns out, when I put on the vampire essence, Kristen's purse was on the bookstore counter, so it didn't disappear when she did. I'd brought it with me when I left. I dug through it till I found her wallet, with her Visa and her Nordstrom's credit card still in it. Time for some new shoes.

I'd never really been shopping before, since my clothes came out of the same magical essence I was made from. I wondered if by some miracle Kristen and I wore the same size shoe, so that if I bought a pair, she could keep them. I didn't feel cocky or tough or any of the things I was used to feeling when I came out to fight vampires. I was tired and sad and a little overwhelmed by the range of bright colors and pretty things that I saw in the windows as I walked by. It was a lot to take in.

I found the perfect pair of shoes at Nordstrom's. The salesclerk promised me that they had a lenient return policy, so I figured if they didn't fit Kristen, she could always bring them back. I hoped they fit her, though, because I knew she was likely to exchange them for a pair of clogs or something equally ugly. The shoes were black patent leather pumps with a platform sole and stiletto heels. Yeah. Much fiercer than anything I'd ever known her to wear. The salesclerk tucked them into their box, wrapped them in silver tissue paper, and put them in a glossy red bag with Nordstrom's on it in white block letters. The bag even had white cord handles. Amazing.

About four p.m. I filled the gas tank in North Seattle then called the vet to check on Petunia —they didn't know Kristen well enough to recognize the difference in my voice. Then I drove out as far west as I could go, following roads that ran roughly along the Puget Sound. The sun was heading towards the horizon, flaring over the tops of the Olympic Mountains, but it was still a while till sunset.

There was a Dick's Drive-In in the Wallingford neighborhood, so I stopped there for dinner. Miles away from the one near Kristen's house, still the food was the same mix of grease and salt that we loved. It didn't seem odd that I had Kristen's knowledge of the Seattle area. I was worried sick about Petunia, too. I washed down my burger with a coke instead of a shake, figuring I could use the caffeine more than the cholesterol, then went back for another order of fries. If I died tonight, we might as well both be happy.

After dinner I traveled surface streets, exploring the Seattle neighborhoods Kristen had heard about but never been to before, catching glimpses of normal people doing normal things like watering flowerbeds and taking after-dinner walks. I used to be normal, or at least Kristen used to be. It was all starting to blur. When evening finally moved towards night, I looked for Lake City Way and went north. It would eventually get me to the Bothell-Everett highway. And home.

Except I wasn't going home. I turned left at the light before the Safeway and stopped in front of the dark mid-century rambler that sat in the middle of a large lot. Shakespeare. If anyone could help me, it was him.

I had barely knocked on the back door when he opened it.

"I heard you park," he said, leading me down into the lower level.

"This ends tonight," I whispered.

He stopped in the hall and turned to face me, concern darkening his eyes. "What has happened, my love?"

"Someone poisoned Kristen's cat." I rubbed my face. He moved closer to me but didn't touch me. "Robbie, um, Kristen's friend, says that the focus is a black rock they used as a paperweight. She says Herbert is going to kill Kristen to take me back."

"Robbie seems very well informed."

"She says Herbert likes to boast after sex." Something in my voice made him reach out, but, again, he stopped without actually touching me.

"Where is this black rock?"

"Gone. When Robbie went to get it for Kristen from the office, it was gone. Herbert must have taken it."

"That is unfortunate."

"Yeah," I said, completely without enthusiasm.

"My love, we will find the rock and we will free you. You have my word on it." He bent his head till his forehead rested lightly on mine.

"Thank you."

We waited until the mall was sure to be deserted then went back to the store. Shakespeare drove this time, a black BMW convertible with leather interior and mahogany trim. Vivienne crawled into the tiny back seat without complaining. In fact, she said nothing when Shakespeare told her to come with us. She gave me a long, strange look then kept quiet. I didn't give her much thought after that. There were too many other things to worry about.

The mall was dead, the wide aisles between rows of stores lit only with the minimum lights required for safety. The bookstore was nearly dark. I stood in front of the door, trying to remember where Kristen had hidden the spare key until Vivienne calmly moved me aside and picked the lock. Interesting what you learn if you live long enough. I silenced the alarm system as soon as we were through the door.

Everything looked like it was supposed to. The register was empty and it looked as if Robbie had put out the boxes of new books that had been delivered. There was only one emergency light on in the office—basically a night-light that burned twenty-four/seven. We had a whispered debate about whether to turn the overhead light on. Vivienne stayed in the front of the store to watch for mall security while Shakespeare and I pawed through things looking for the rock.

"It looks like Kristen worked here today," I muttered as I scanned the room. The bookshelves were all in order and there were no piles of packing materials strewn about.

"Nothing looks amiss," Shakespeare said, crouching down to examine the base of one of the bookshelves.

"Well, the level of organization looks weird, because Robbie's usually the queen of clutter."

"She is, isn't she," Herbert said, leaning against the open door and leering at me. He had Robbie around the waist with his fingertips tucked into the top of her pants. She had an arm around him, though it looked like she was using him more for support than affection. Her eyes were shut and her head listed towards his shoulder.

"Master, I didn't see him. He didn't come through the front." Vivienne rushed up behind him.

"Quiet, food," snapped Herbert, pointing at her with his free hand. She clutched at her throat and I could hear the air rasping in and out as she struggled to breath. "Hey, dead guy," he continued. "It's been years. You were extra crispy the last time I saw you."

"And it will be longer before we meet again," Shakespeare said as he moved quickly to stand between Herbert and me.

"Oh yeah, you're going to destroy me, right? Good luck with that." Herbert pulled Robbie in for a kiss, keeping one eye on me while he did it. "Your friend is pretty, or should I say Kristen's friend. She's a naughty girl, though. Surprised me how dirty she could be."

"You're sick," I said.

"No, I'm a demon. Demons come from hell. That makes me one of the bad guys. It's very simple. I control Jai so she can kill vampires."

"Release Jai to me." Shakespeare brought the full force of his compulsive power to the words, making me flinch and Vivienne give a garbled cry. "I hold the focus and I demand her freedom."

"You're bluffing." He released Robbie, and after a momentary stumble she lurched out into the front of the store, trying to get away from him. We followed her.

She only got as far as the mystery shelves. "Stay," Herbert said sharply, and she stopped. "Good girl," he murmured, sliding behind her and running his hands down her sides. He turned her so they were facing us, one hand up under her shirt.

"Now then, you said you had the focus. I don't believe you. Show it to me, and I'll let her go."

I'd never noticed how deranged Herbert's smile could look.

"The focus is safely away from here."

Shakespeare looked supremely confident. I think we both guessed that Herbert didn't have the stone either, or he'd have called Shakespeare's bluff.

The door slammed open, carrying in a gust of vampire smell. Hugh stood in the doorway. He assessed the scene for only a moment then came at me. I ducked back behind a bookshelf and pulled Mr. Sticky from its sheath. Hugh was quicker and had me pushed up against the wall and a dagger under my chin before I could react. Shakespeare dropped down and drew a blade from a sheath on his calf. Vivienne screamed.

"This one is for the Queen," Hugh said, his voice gone flat and hollow.

"Brother, leave her," Shakespeare said.

"No," he roared and pushed the knife in far enough to draw blood.

Shakespeare darted around the bookshelf, knocking it into Hugh. That gave me a step toward freedom, one that I wasn't able to take advantage of. While Shakespeare and Hugh thrashed through the store, their attention on each other, Herbert appeared in front of me. He held a string of garlic and a really long knife.

"Recognize this?" he asked, raising the garlic. "I borrowed it the night I broke in to throw knives at your pillow. Or was it the other night when....well, never mind. It's here now and you're going to turn into Kristen and I'm going to kill her and then Jai will go back to being a good girl. And there's really nothing you can do about it."

He raised his eyebrows and drew his lips back over his big front teeth, but it really wasn't a smile. It made me sick. He held the garlic towards me. I pointed Mr. Sticky at him.

"Oh, that. Well, it's a demon blade. See?" He waved his hand and Mr. Sticky faded away. "No weapon, no memory of how to fight, and no real reason to want to stick around. Poor Jai. Put the garlic on."

I threw myself sideways, just in time for Hugh to come around the corner and grab me from behind. Shakespeare was too far away, and by the time he got there my arms were pinned and one side of my face was mashed into the bookcase on the back wall. The corner of a hardcover was up my nose and the point of Hugh's dagger was at my back.

"Good vampire, that's right," Herbert said. "Now, hold her so I can get the garlic around her neck."

"Anybody move and I'll kill her," Hugh gasped, looking wildly from Shakespeare to Herbert and back. My shoulders screamed in their sockets and I could feel another thin slice where the blade caught my skin.

"Let her go, Hugh." Shakespeare was the only one of them that sounded at all sane. Robbie staggered over to Herbert and pulled on the arm that held the knife.

"Can't kill Kristen," she mumbled.

"Get the fuck off me," he shouted, and cuffed her upside the head with his fist. She crumbled at his feet.

"Well isn't this a pretty tableau," said a voice from the doorway. The Queen sauntered into the room, a row of pretty young vampires arrayed around her. She was dressed in black, a beaded drop-waist dress that should have looked harsh on her frosted rose complexion and instead made her look like a dream. She had a thick headband worn across her brow with a cluster of feathers and beads at one temple. One black feather ran down the side of her face to her chin. A thick string of pearls hung down to her waist, echoing the cool perfection of her skin. "Don't go near the girl," she said over her shoulder to her entourage. "I don't want to lose any of you."

"My Lady," Shakespeare recovered himself and nodded towards her.

"Sir John." She returned his nod. "You seem to have your hands full."

"Yes, my Lady. I am attempting to free Jai from the demon."

"Steal her away from me? No fucking way." Herbert kicked Robbie out of the way and took several steps towards Shakespeare.

"Quiet, demon." The Queen pointed at him and he froze in place.

"Now, continue your explanation. Oh, and Sir Hugh, what a surprise. Release the girl."

"My Queen, I bring her to you as an offering," Hugh said, pulling me tighter against his body. "We will savor her together,"

"Release her before I kill you," the Queen snapped. Hugh fell back and I slumped down the bookcase to the floor. "Better. Now, Sir John?"

"The demon was threatening the life of her current hostess." Shakespeare said. "He aimed to kill Kristen in order to take Jai away."

Herbert grunted and struggled, stuck by the Queen's magic.

The Queen took several steps towards me. "And what does Jai want to do?"

I sat up slowly, gently pulling my shoulders back and forth, trying to loosen them. One hand wiped at the blood that was dripping down my chest from Hugh's blade.

"Don't tease me child," the Queen murmured as she watched my fingers smear blood across my bare skin. "The smell of you is already hard to resist. Tell me what you want."

"I want to know who I am."

"That's it? That's all? Not money, fame, or fortune? Come on now. Ask for anything."

I smiled at her, wondering why I thought someone so blindingly powerful was my ally. "That's it."

She tilted her head to one side, giving me an appraising stare. The feather cupped her face like the wing of a crow. "Well, hell, that's easy. We'll destroy the demon, Shakespeare can hold your focus, and you can wear that vial of vampire essence to keep your hostess underground."

"Not so easy, my Queen. I do not have the focus, nor, I believe, does the demon."

"And I think Kristen's ready to give up being my hostess," I added.

The Queen gave an artificially deep sigh. "Really, you should really be more careful with powerful objects like this," she said, and held up the focus. Herbert gave a strangled squeak. "Shut up, demon. Why did the demonaya put a third rate shapeshifter like you in charge of Jai anyway, and what's that thing at your feet?"

Herbert screamed, rage whistling through him like a distant teakettle.

"It's your slut, isn't it?" The Queen laughed. "I hope you haven't eaten too much of her soul. I don't want to destroy her when I unbind the spell that keeps you intact. She probably wouldn't deserve it, and if she rises as a zombie it will be so upsetting to her friends."

The Queen smiled as if she thought she'd said something funny, and walked towards me through the bookshelves, her courtiers stalking behind her like models on a catwalk. "I'm going to call your hostess, Jai, and ask her whether she's ready to give you up. The demon is right about this much. If she doesn't do it willingly, I'll have to kill her."

"Don't," I said. "If she's not ready, I'll wait till she is."

"That's very sweet, but there are things I need you to do. Sir John promised that the two of you would be my allies. I'm going to hold you to that."

"My Queen, I brought her to you. What is my reward?"

"Shut up, Hugh. You'll get your reward...privately." She gave him a look that got close to Herbert's level of twisted. Hugh groaned. "You don't know anything about a vampire trying to make children, do you? A vampire who's not quite powerful enough, so the children turn out feral?"

"Lady—Lady Merli—Merliadne—" Hugh stammered.

"Sir John, I apologize for accusing you. Had I known your brother was here—" She walked over to Hugh and stuck a long-nailed finger into his chest. "I have destroyed vampires for less, Hugh Robartes."

"No, it wasn't me." He managed to gasp the words, terror distorting his face.

"You didn't present yourself to me when you arrived. That alone will bring punishment. Do not move. I will deal with you later." She spun on her heals and faced me. "When I lay my hands on your head, it will bring your hostess."

I bent forward slightly so the Queen could reach me. As soon as she touched me Jai melted into Kristen—a weary Kristen wearing Birkenstocks, a denim skirt and bloody tee shirt, her hair a wild tangle of frizz.

My glasses were missing, and I blinked a couple times to bring the room into focus.

"Lady Kristen," Shakespeare bowed to me.

"Hi Shakespeare, um, Sir John, I guess. Oh my gosh, Robbie," I groaned and dropped to my knees.

"Don't touch her," the Queen said. "The demon's power is running through her and I don't want it to contaminate you."

I choked back a sob and stood up.

"Lady Kristen, we are trying to determine the best course for Jai's future. Are you still happy being her hostess, or are you ready to give her up?" Sir John asked.

I took a deep breath before answering. "That's a hard question. I'd hate for her to get dumped into whichever random girl Herbert can find. I can tell she wants to be with you, Sir John."

"Herbert will not be involved in Jai's future," said the Queen, smiling maliciously in the demon's direction.

"Good. That's good. You know, I think Jai deserves more than I can give her. It's no wonder she can't remember who she is when she only comes out long enough to kill a vamp every week or so."

"You are correct in that," said Sir John. His face was so carefully expressionless that even I could see how much he was holding back.

"I mean, I've got the bookstore and, well, there's this guy—sort of. I'd have to give all that up for her to have a real life."

"That would be difficult for you," he said.

"Yeah, so, I guess, as long as she's going to a good hostess, it's time for me to give her up." My eyes filled with tears faster than I could blink them away.

Sir John bowed to me again. "You are a wise woman, Lady Kristen."

"That's settled then. We have the focus and the current hostess is willing. All we need now is a new hostess. I assume you have a candidate, Sir John."

I was confused for a minute, wondering where things were going.

"Vivienne?"

No one responded. "Vivienne?" he asked again.

"Dizzy looking gal that's kinda sepia-toned and smells like roses?" one of the young vampires in the Queen's entourage asked.

"I believe so, yes," Sir John said.

"She left a few minutes ago. 'Bout the time our Lady M nailed your brother for making ferals."

"Well," the Queen said with a sly grin. "This is an interesting wrinkle." She wandered in the direction of the bestseller display, where she could run a hand over the chest of one of the handsome vamps she had in tow. "I could fix it, you know," she said with her back to the rest of us. "But it will cost you, John."

"By my word, my Lady, I would be open to your ideas," Sir John said, his voice wooden.

"The second thing on our to-do list tonight was to destroy a feral that we found. We were going to toss her out into the sun right after it rose and watch her burn." Several of the young vampires smiled at the Queen as she spoke. "She's out in the limo right now, a little dirty and completely mindless. We could put Jai in her."

"Jai would be a vampire," I said, louder than I'd meant to.

"No," the Queen turned and waved a hand at me. "The feral would be a hostess, just like any other. It would just give Jai the freedom to remain in place indefinitely. Sir John?"

"I am uncertain. Perhaps we should ask Jai herself."

The Queen rolled her eyes, then came over and put her hands on my head. I swear it burned when she touched me, though the feeling faded as Jai took over.

"I've been listening," I said. "I wouldn't be a vampire in truth, and I would like staying in the same hostess."

"I believe you would gain even more strength and agility," Shakespeare said.

"I'd have to eat blood? From strangers?"

"To a certain extent, we can sustain each other, but yes, you will need others. There's always Vivienne..." He looked away but not before I saw the hope in his face.

Solving one problem created a bunch of others. I shut my eyes. When I opened them again, the Queen was staring at me. I could feel her digging under my surface. Creepy.

"And so on and so forth," the Queen said. "Go get her," she pointed at two of her minions. "I will hold the focus, John, until you earn it back."

Before the Queen made the switch, she looked over at Herbert. "*Adnihilo, dispersus inter astrum.*" She flicked her fingers at him and he vanished. Robbie gave a low moan. Hugh shuddered. Even Shakespeare looked impressed by her show.

"Don't move," the Queen said, standing in front of me with the stone in her hands. "I draw the djin from you and place it here." It felt like she'd pulled a spider's web out of me, and I fell back a step.

"Bring the thing here," she told her minions, and, one on each arm, they dragged the feral vampire over next to me. She hadn't been a vampire long; her jeans had once been expensive and her long hair hung in dirty pre-dreadlock ropes down her back. The Queen placed the stone on the feral vampire's forehead. The thing thrashed and fought to get away. "Hold it still," she said through gritted teeth, glaring at the young vampires.

And then it was done. Jai was standing in the feral vampire's place. She was slimmer than what I remembered seeing in the mirror, with a slightly smaller bustline and narrower hips. Instead of the skimpy black dress, she had on a pair of tailored tan capris-length slacks and a crisp white camp shirt. It was unbuttoned enough to show a fair amount of cleavage, and from the right angle a glimpse of lace-trimmed bra. She was way more grown-up than I'd seen before, though she still had the cheekbones, the eyes, and the gorgeous thick hair. She looked at Shakespeare and smiled, and then she turned to me, her eyes full of many different emotions

"Kristen."

"Jai, you look so different. Nice, I mean, beautiful, really, but different."

"I'm always a blend, you know, of the parts that are me and the parts that are the hostess." She shrugged. "This woman was probably older than you."

"So I gave you the sleaze factor."

"I guess you did." She grinned broadly. "Something for you to think about."

"Wow. Just, wow."

"Keep her safe, Sir John," the Queen said. "Until she can manage her new desires. Jai, I will have need of you very soon." She walked over to Hugh. When she reached for him, he whimpered and flinched. She grabbed his arm hard enough to tear through the fabric of his shirt. Her entourage followed her out of the store.

"Help me, John," we heard Hugh cry out as they headed up the mall.

Shakespeare didn't watch them go, nor did he move when he heard his brother's voice.

He and Jai hadn't touched each other yet, but there was enough heat between them that I wanted to give them some privacy. The best I could do was push them out of the store. I locked up then checked Robbie's pulse. She was still alive, which was something. Maybe I could get her on a bus, pretending she was my drunken friend. First, I needed some sleep. I lay down next to her, using her belly for a pillow, and stared into the weird electronic twilight that was the mall at night until I fell asleep.

EPILOGUE

The store stayed closed for three days. I called the police and reported the vandalism. On the third morning, I put an ad on Craig's List, looking for some part-time help. On the fourth day, I got to work at nine-thirty. The first email I got was from Mall management, threatening to evict me if I didn't open back up. The second was from Corey, checking to make sure I was feeling better after my bout with the flu.

At noon that day Robbie showed up. She'd come from a lawyer's office where she'd filled out the paperwork to file for separation from Doug. He'd been basically living at Microsoft for the last year or so, so we weren't sure he'd even notice. Whenever she gets drunk, she calls me and says that she never thought she'd be the type of girl who slept around on her husband. If she's really drunk, she tries to tell me some of the things Herbert made her do. As much as I love her, I *so* don't want to know.

I went ahead and hired a part-time salesclerk. Robbie's working more hours and says that when the divorce is final she wants to use some of the Doug's Microsoft money to buy into the business. I think there are trust issues to work through before we do that. If Herbert really did eat part of her soul, she doesn't seem to have missed it. She's still my best friend.

Don't know what that says about either of us.

The part-time help guarantees me one day off a week, which is huge. The downside is that there'll be even less money for savings and I'll have to take a pay cut. Corey is hinting that my expenses would be lower if I moved in with him. Not yet. There's Petunia to consider, now that she's recovered, because Corey's not a cat fan. He's got big plans for my days off, mostly involving the great outdoors. I told him I'd only hike on flat surfaces, which is kind of limiting when you live between two mountain ranges. We're working it out.

Shakespeare and Jai turned up one night with a gift for me. It was a pair of the most gorgeous black pumps ever. Jai said she bought them on my Nordstrom's card, but I never saw the charge on my statement. I got myself a little black dress that is cut lower in the front and higher in the hem than anything I'd ever owned. I wore the dress and shoes to a Microsoft function, and Corey spent the entire evening trying to nibble on my neck. Woo baby. He renamed one of his Pandora stations for me, the one that plays only his favorite music. If that's not commitment, I don't know what is.

"Jai." John's voice was a soft rumble against my back.

"Hmmm..." I sighed, tugging one of John's arms closer around me. It felt so good to have his hand cupping my breast and to feel him twisting my nipple between his fingers. His spicy incense scent was like a drug.

"Awake again?" he breathed against my cheek. I reveled in the softness of his lips, the hardness of other things.

"Ready again," I giggled and rolled him onto his back, straddling him, sliding him in. "And this time, I'm hungry."

He gave me a look that that warmed me up from head to toe as I pinned his arms above his head. He was all there in front of me, the dead dark bits and the beautiful golden threads. I ran my tongue along the tips of my fangs, leaned forward, and bit.

The End

ABOUT THE AUTHOR

Liv Rancourt is a writer of speculative fiction and romance. She lives in Seattle with her husband, two teenagers, two cats and one wayward puppy. She finds writing stories that have happy endings is a way to good balance her work in the neonatal intensive care unit, and is thrilled to be publishing her first novella with Black Opal Books.

Visit Liv on her website at: http://www.livrancourt.com